Gnomes and Knights

A collection of short stories both whimsical and heroic

Michael Parkes

Cover art by Raeann Stambulic

ISBN: 9798484806584

Thanks to Raeann Stambulic for being a great editor, cover artist, and endlessly supportive of my second book. Also, thanks to Nancy Mohammed for proof reading, and thanks to Nikki Lyndt Burchell for giving her thoughts on some stories in Gnomes.

"Nibbity, Nobbity, Sorcerous Gnome!"
     -Fredrick Jerome Kopillus Gnome

Table of Contents

Gnomes:

Nathan the Knight:

Book 1
Gnomes

Story 1
The Gnome, the Mole and the Garden

The garden of Gertrude Grips, though Gertie is how she preferred to be known, was a well-maintained and gorgeous space behind her home. Everyone in the neighbourhood always had a lawn to water or a greeting to say, and it made all those who lived there so happy each day. None among them were better than Gertie at that, who was a little old lady often dressed in billowy yellow slacks, a sleeveless pink blouse and a floppy khaki sunhat. Her and her husband, George Grips, had lived there in marital bliss since they bought the yellow brick home back in 1966; each morning began with a loving kiss. But this story isn't about the nice old lady who likes to garden or her kind old husband who likes to collect stamps. Nor is it about Jason down the street who likes lava lamps, Ted watering his lawn just a few houses down, or Laurie on the next street over who's new to town. It's actually about what lives in the garden itself, not a brownie or fairy or dryad or elf, but rather the one whom within makes his home; a rather silly little magical gnome.

Past the decorative cranes and the tulips and rose bushes, around the tree and just out of view - unless you went back there and looked at it just the right way - was an itty-bitty door in the trunk, clear as day. Gertie assumed it was one of her countless lawn ornaments that she'd forgotten placing there, though to be fair, if you opened the door, nothing was there. That is, of course, unless the special words were said as you tapped the door three times: "Nibbity, Nobbity, Sorcerous Gnome!" Upon uttering the words and tapping the door, ancient gnomish sorcery would shoot throughout the tree, revealing a cute and quaint little home; the unmistakable burrow of a certain gnome. There were bits and baubles and odds and ends, and of course, there were also a couple thing-a-ma-jigs and even a few whats-a-ma-whos-its, to whatever end.

These things belonged to Fredrick Jerome Kopillus Gnome, the friendly and wonderful creature who dwelt in that home. He was shortish and squattish and rather rotund; a white beard on his face, a red cap on his head, and rather than going barefoot, he wore big boots instead. He was happy and helpful and all full of glee, and he lived in the burrow right under the tree. Fredrick Jerome Kopillus Gnome - though usually just Fred was how he was known - was the guardian of the garden and the lord of the land; though lord of just the garden, I hope you understand. He politely asked the squirrel, Sydney Squeaks, to not eat the flowers, and took up watch after sunset into the dark nighttime hours. He slept in the morning and held his vigil at night, that way Gertie didn't see him; it would give her a fright. So was the duty of Fred the Gnome, and under the tree was his cute little home. All was well and all was grand, until a rather adventurous mole found his way onto the land.

The mole was greyish and squinty; he dug here and dug there. He just wanted to find a nice place for his lair. He dug and he dug, soon making his way to the garden of Gertie Grips as the sun set that day. It was a beautiful night, and the garden resplendent, but what really sold him were the tulips and rose bushes that made it transcendent! It was then he knew what he had to do; he, Morris Montgomery Mortimer the Mole, would live there in a nice cozy hole. That made finding a place to dig it his new goal, so he looked to the right, then looked to the left, then looked at the tree looming above him instead. It was big and tall and leafy and shady, the most perfect of places for a quiet residence, maybe. He got out of his tunnel and canvassed the land; the front was too lumpy and the sides were too bland. What really spoke to him was the back of the tree, it was quiet and cozy and there was even space free! He dug and he dug and he dug a bit more, until Fred the Gnome gave a great roar!

"Hey! What are you doing?" he indignantly squeaked, "You're digging a hole too close to my tree!" Now Morris the Mole could not hear very well, so he kept on digging where he wished to dwell. Fred wouldn't have it, he wouldn't, he simply could not! He stomped his big boots and felt his face get hot, "You stop it, you quit it, you cease this at once!"

Upon hearing the shouting, Morris the Mole stopped digging and swivelled around, and came face to face with a gnome stomping around. He was shortish and squattish and had a white beard, and Morris the Mole wondered when he had appeared.

"Well, hail and hello, my windy little fellow, it harshens my vibe that you are not mellow."

Fred the Gnome, quite red in the face, couldn't at all stand this flagrant disgrace!

"You're digging a hole on dear old Gertie's lawn! More importantly, that's my home your dirt's piling on!" Indeed, there was, quite plain to see, a mound of dirt piled high on the door in the tree.

"Oh goodness, oh golly, oh heck and oh jeez! I'm sorry I didn't see the door in this tree! I didn't realize I was intruding on your land: we moles aren't great at inferring things; I hope you understand. Again, I'm sorry that I made you sour, I simply wanted a place to sleep in the daytime hours. I know we just met and I caused a big mess, I'm sorry and ashamed to have caused you stress, but would you consider a neighbour? I'm quiet and friendly and really quite dear. I could clear the dirt off your door and then dig away from here."

His dirty clawed paw pointed the opposite way, to a nice spot under the shed that was a fair bit away. It wouldn't be noticed by Gertie at all! Maybe a neighbour would be nice after all...

Fred thought of it fast, then he said all polite, "Well really, I'm sorry for being so uptight. Watch the garden with me and I don't see an issue, we hold vigil at night and I'd love to do it with you!"

So, it was decided and together they worked. Clearing off the door to the burrow was first, then together they dug a den under the shed, and that's the story of how Morris met Fred.

Story 2
The Ants and the Plants

Fredrick Jerome Kopillus Gnome was peacefully sleeping inside his home. He was snoring while snoozing and sleeping while dreaming, though outside his burrow the garden was teeming. Not with flowers, and not with plants. The garden was filled with an army of ants!

Fredrick Jerome Kopillus Gnome, though usually just Fred was how he was known, was the guardian of the garden and the lord of the land, though lord of just the garden, I hope you understand. His partner in vigil was Morris the Mole, his friend and his neighbour who lived in a hole. Not by the tree, as there dwelt Fred, rather Morris the Mole lived under the shed. It was their job, well more like their duty, to ensure the garden was allowed to grow smoothly. They warded off Sydney Squeaks trying to eat the flowers, though they offered her shelter during harsh thundershowers. They watered and weeded and protected and guarded. It's why the garden of Gertie was so well regarded! Imagine their horror and their shock at the ants! The dastardly insects were eating the plants!

Fred opened his door and noticed something was amiss! There was nothing that could have prepared him for this! The tulips, the roses, the shrubs and the hedges. All the beautiful plants were gnawed on the edges! Now this wouldn't pass and this wouldn't stand! Not while Fred the Gnome was lord of the land! He scrambled over to the hole of Morris; his heart filled with dread. Luckily Morris lived just under the shed.

"Morris, oh Morris, my neighbour and friend! All the leaves in the garden are gnawed on the ends! Who could have done this? It's so mean and so dirty! Worse still is the effect it'll have on dear old Gertie!"

Now Gertie was lovely, a joy all around. Typically, within the garden is where she could be found. She wore billowy yellow slacks and a pink sleeveless blouse, paired with a floppy khaki sunhat when she was working outside of the house. Gertie's Garden was her pride and joy; the gnawed ends of the leaves would do much more than annoy. The gnome and the mole worked on the garden at night, because seeing a gnome during the day would give Gertie a fright. It

9

was home for all three of them; gnome, human and mole, and stopping the ants would be their shared goal. But would she be angry? Would she pitch a fit? Fred wondered how Gertie would react to it.

"No need to worry," reasoned Morris the Mole. "Why don't we just explain to the ants that it takes a great toll? How we love the garden and so does Gertie, and why gnawing the leaves is so mean and dirty?"

Fred the Gnome considered the matter. Would the ants actually listen to their pleas or would they consider it blather? Would they march onward and eat everything in sight? That would be a horrible plight! Not one to sit idle, and out of duty to his home, a parlay was agreed upon by Fred the Gnome. He and Morris surveyed the plants, and noted the extent of the actions of the ants. Then off they wandered, in the dead of the night, to find the troop of ants and make this wrong right.

They crept through the bushes and flowers and plants, because somewhere in the large garden must lurk the ants. It took them a short while before they found it: a rather sandy hill with ants all around it!

10

They walked up to the structure and asked for the queen, and in short order a large ant could be seen. She had a vanguard of about twenty or thirty, and unlike her workers she was clean and not dirty. But the worst of the worst, it nearly caused Fred to do an angry dance, was that she was munching on a leaf from the plants!

All red in the face at the sight of this disgrace, Fred had to stop himself from stomping all over the place. He put on a smile, gave a wave with his hand, and said, "Hello there! I'm Fred the Gnome, protector and guardian of this beautiful land that we all call home."

Morris the Mole gave also offered a wave and a hearty hello; he might be a mole but he was still a friendly fellow. The queen looked up at Morris, then back to Fred, then down at the leaf that she was being fed.

Fred thought she understood the matter. But just to be sure, and just to be clear, he asked her, "Could your ants not eat the leaves from around here? Why, this garden's dear old Gertie's pride and joy! To deny her happiness because you all needed a snack, I'm sorry to say, I can't abide that!"

The queen nodded curtly as she started to speak, "Now just who are you to issue orders to me? I'm the queen of my subjects and they shall do as they please! We need food and that's provided by the abundance of leaves! I must feed my subjects, or surely, they'll starve! I'm sorry, but there's no other food in this yard!"

Fred the Gnome thought for a minute, then after a bit of thinking, he had an idea to fix it! "Now wait just one moment, I think I know what to do! There's an old gnomish spell that I think we could use! I can cause a tree to bear fruit, to feed you and your ants, that way you won't have to spoil the plants! A few days ago, Gertie planted a tree by your hill; I'll enchant that one since it's young still. This way the problem is solved, we can part ways as friends, because rather than leaves, you'll have apples instead!"

The queen happily chittered and agreed at once! Apples and gnomish sorcery sure sounded like fun! She watched as Fred brewed a magical potion, that looked an awful lot like calamine lotion. He then gathered it up, poured it onto the roots, and wouldn't you know it, he started chanting to boot!

"Nibbity, Nobbity, Sorcerous Gnome! Let this young tree be enchanted by Fredrick the Gnome! Let it bear fruit, and let it be sweet! Turn this young sapling into an apple tree!" His beard flew about and there was a sparkle of gnomish magic, then everything suddenly became less dramatic. The tree sprouted green buds that quickly turned red, about the same colour of the hat worn by Fred. They grew and they fell and they bounced on the ground. The apples as promised were laying all around!

The ants were happy and started to cheer! There would be apples for many years! From that point on the leaves were un-gnawed; it turned out the ants preferred apple sauce.

Story 3
Gertie's Garden

At 342 Hubert Drive lived a cute little gnome, Fredrick the Gnome is how he was known. He was the guardian of the garden and the lord of the land, though lord of just the garden, I hope you understand. Though rather than Fred, this story is about another. A wonderful lady and beloved grandmother. That's right, rather than Fred and Morris rushing to save the garden in a hurry, this story centres on George and Gertie!

Behind the yellow brick house of 342 Hubert Drive, the garden was always so colourful and alive. Perhaps it was the tulips or roses or simply the colours, but clearly Gertie was great at tending her flowers. Vivacious and vivid and very bright green, anything in that garden was a sight to be seen! If Fred was the lord of the land, then Gertie was the queen! She knew there was something special in her garden, though it was unseen. Long had she suspected something magic at play, though exactly what it was, Gertie could not say. The leaves' edges were gnawed once, but then it stopped, and no squirrel ever seemed to eat her flower tops. What exactly was there was not clear to her, and there was certainly nothing that George could infer. It seemed as if something or someone looked out for the plants, though just who would do that wasn't evident at first glance. Gertie wondered what safeguarded her garden, but she thought it was probably just all the work she put in that made it so well regarded. Yet the unshakeable feeling of something guarding her garden never quite left her mind once it had started.

It was a couple days after she'd planted a tree, and after fresh red apples all around could be seen, that she had her proof there was magic afoot! A tiny wee sapling that bore fruit overnight? Gertie knew then that something wasn't quite right. There was no malice, but certainly some sort of power, and perhaps that is what safeguarded her flowers. She was out in the garden for hours during the day, but maybe at night the guardian of the garden came out to play?

Gertie thought about staying up to catch a glimpse of the critter at night, but she thought George would think something wasn't quite right. "Georgie, my love, I shall come to bed soon, but I simply must find out what the magic creature in my garden shall do. He comes out at night and sleeps during the day. No, I'm not crazy, why's that something you'd say?"

So rather than that she needed a plan, perhaps a camera to snap an image of the critter on her land? Or maybe a trap, a net and some bait? Then suddenly Gertie thought of something great! A note and a cookie, why that was the plan! When it came to Gertie's cookies everyone was a fan. She could leave out a plate around 7 or 8 and place a note beside it to communicate! Why yes, that would work, why that would be great! So before going to bed she set out a note and a plate. It simply read: Hello neighbour, it's me dear old Gertie! Just wanted to say hi without being wordy. After she did and she went inside, she could have sworn she saw the gleaming of eyes.

Come the next morning, the cookies were gone! The note was still there, but something was tacked on. It looked kind of funny, and it shone in the air. It looked like a glyph had been scribed onto there. Gertie ran her finger over it, then with a burst of magic, before

Gertie's eyes a cookie-shaped puff of smoke floated past them. It hung in the air for a second or two, then faded away, though the air still smelled like cookies, Gertie was inclined to say. She didn't want to disturb whatever was there, for it seemed friendly and like it might even care. From that point on Gertie never again bothered the guardian of the garden, though she left out cookies every so often. After all, she wanted whatever was there to know they were appreciated, and leaving out cookies seemed a fair way to say it.

Story 4
Gary the Gremlin

Gertie's Garden at 342 Hubert Drive was always so beautiful, green and alive! Morris and Fred lived there in bliss, in their minds there was nowhere more gorgeous than this! The flowers were bright, the grass was green, truly the garden was a sight to be seen! Yet just next door was a very different garden. Its grass was yellow and its plants were dead; it was a rather grim place if you asked Fred. The people who lived there were angry and vile, and no one had tended the plants in a while. Rather than a gnome, a gremlin dwelt there, though he lived not in a cozy burrow; rather he dwelt in a lair.

Gary the Gremlin was the lord of that land, a rather bleak occupation; why he would want that was not easy to understand. Specifically, under a rock pile was where he dwelt, and being a gremlin, he actually liked how the area smelled. There were old dead bushes and rotting vines, but to Gary the Gremlin it all smelled divine! Unlike Fred the Gnome, who was rotund and gleeful, Gary the Gremlin looked downright evil. He was scrawny and pointy and his voice was a hiss. His brown baggy clothes hung off his frame, and he wasn't really one to ever play games. Rather than guard the garden he saw himself as its master, and he was always looking for ways to make it rot faster. He invited in worms and slugs and snails, anything nasty that would leave a slime trail. His repugnant brown garden was also home to many insects, from bloodsuckers to plant munchers to beetles with massive forceps.

Anything vile was welcome amongst the rotting plants and dirty rocks, though Gary's main focus was actually stealing socks. No protein at breakfast would see your socks stolen, ditto if you didn't take a shower or eat enough fibre, or really any other reason a gremlin so desired. It was passed down from generation to generation that the stealing of socks was a gremlin's main occupation. You see gremlins, like gnomes, are magical creatures, but rather than being helpful they possessed more spiteful natures. While Fred could sprout flowers with a wave of his hand, Gary much preferred to blight the land.

So, as you can infer, Gary was rather unpleasant, though the rather rough family was why he was present. Gertie attracted Fred to her garden because she was so mild; whereas Gary was drawn to his rock pile because Gertie's neighbours were beyond vile. Gnomes and gremlins were both attracted by people's actions and thoughts, and they dwelt where they found them, if there were a lot. Gnomes liked kindness but gremlins were drawn to evil, and they both preferred to live near their respective people.

Gary had dwelt there for a number of years, and the number of socks he'd accumulated was giving him fears. He had a whole vault under his rock pile, and at first the huge number of socks had made him smile. But now it made him worry, what was he to do? His vault was overflowing and he was running out of room! He'd have to think of something, and think of it soon! He wondered if Fred would help him out, though there would be contention, of that he had no doubt. You see, gremlins and gnomes are sworn enemies, mostly because of their opinions on trees. Gnomes like large vibrant oaks growing in peaceful dells, whereas gremlins much preferred rotting trees in which to dwell, even better if there was a strong smelly smell. It may seem silly, and perhaps it was, but gremlins and gnomes were divided and trees were the cause.

Gary dismissed the feeling and decided that day, "The gnome of Gertie's Garden shall agree to help or I'll be dismayed! He's so helpful and happy what else could he say?" Where else was Gary to turn? Fred was the only magical being nearby who'd understand his concern.

It was so vivid and green! It was so ugly and vile! This garden didn't even have a rock pile! Gary suppressed a gag and continued on his path, though the tulips and roses made him want to turn back. This whole place was so ugly, the lawn ornaments were too shiny and clean, it was to the point Gary found it obscene!

Behind a great oak neither rotted nor strong smelling, he found the little door to Fred's personal dwelling. He knocked, knocked again, then knocked a bit more, until Fred the Gnome himself answered the door. He was rotund and gleeful and he had a red hat, though Gary never understood why he chose to wear that. Nevertheless, he was here for a reason, so for now he'd avoid any teasing.

"Hello Fred, it's me, your neighbour Gary. I have a small problem that I find kind of scary. You see, I have so many socks that I've run out of space! I wondered if you might have a solution for the problem I face?"

Fred's face darkened and he said with a sneer, "What made you think to come here? Leave this place at once! If you think I'd help you, then you're a dunce!"

Gary glared back and replied with a shout, "You think I like asking gnomes for help? If I wasn't so desperate, I'd handle it myself! You know my magic can't create, just destroy! That's why I came here, not to blight, not to toy!"

Fred thought on it a moment, then decided to lend aid. If he was in this situation, he'd hope Gary would do the same. "I guess I'll try to help, but only this once! I hope after this I don't see you for months!"

Gary the Gremlin took offence; to be spoken down to by a gnome? Fred was lucky he even thought to come to his home!

"Now you listen here you ridiculous creature! I'm not exactly having fun with this either! Why do gremlins and gnomes even hate each other? I've never done any wrong to you or your kin! I demand to be respected! My patience wears thin!"

Fred the Gnome thought on that thought. All gremlins were evil, were they not? Or was it just perhaps how they were treated? If Fred was viewed as a villain, would that not cause him to become mean and conceited? Would he be sour and dour and angry and rude? Perhaps gremlins aren't all evil and it was just the gnomish attitude?

With a sheepish look, and an awkward grin, Fred the Gnome said, "How silly I have been! It was wrong of me to judge you so fast! Preconceived notions because of our preference of plants? A rotting log, a healthy tree, it really is nonsense! Please forgive me for my disrespectful comments! Show me your sock vault, I'll show you respect, and perhaps we can talk about our opinions on plants?"

Gary was stunned, he was shocked and appalled! Never had dealings with gnomes gone so amazingly well! He was flustered and stammered; he really didn't know what to say! He'd have to tell the other gremlins that crossed his path of this fateful day!

"I don't know how to respond; we gremlins are rarely shown kindness! Normally we're shunned because we like rotting leaves and crawling bugs, and we're not really the type to give many hugs. I know we're seen as evil but give me a chance! I promise not to blight any of Gertie's plants!"

And so off they went, crossing through the vibrant green garden, then over the fence and under the rocks. Gary the Gremlin was finally getting help with his socks!

Now Fred was surprised, this was an amazing burrow! The sheer size and the details caused his brow to furrow!

There were sparkles of red magic that clung to the ceiling like bats, about the same shade of red as Fred's hat. Rocks were incorporated into pillars and columns, and it looked like Gary even had a stone golem! It looked like an inuksuk that tended the lair, though it seemed Gary had given it a shock of red hair.

"Gary this is amazing! How did you do this?" Fred was so flabbergasted he was rendered clueless!

Gary just shrugged and answered the question, "We gremlins view creating elaborate burrows as one of our main occupations. We steal socks, make burrows, and as you know our magic is more about curses than creation, which I always found tragic. But what is a curse if not just a spiteful enchantment? So, I assembled some stones, and it took a few tries, but then they shifted and moved before my eyes! I had made a golem! But he had no hair, and I thought he might want some to stay warm in my lair. One more curse that causes hair to sprout, and then he was ready to be my guard and keep intruders out."

"Gary, that's amazing beyond compare! We gnomes don't have any stone golems in our lairs! I guess we tend to call them burrows, but still, that's so neat! Enchanting stones like that is an amazing feat! I made a tree bear fruit once but that seems like nothing to what you've achieved!"

"I suppose I could show you how to go about it, and I suppose if we both know enchanting, then we have common ground. But come, let me show you where my problem is found."

In the back of the lair was a large door, Fred wondered how he hadn't noticed it before. Gary waved his hand, and wide open it flung! Socks spilled everywhere and Fred came to see why Gary needed his intervention, there were so many socks like you couldn't imagine; so many, too many, far too many socks! Fred stared at the enormous pile, wide-eyed in shock.

"So, you see my problem," said Gary the Gremlin, "Too many socks with nowhere to put them. I could throw some out, or give them away? Though I wouldn't know to whom, nor what I would say."

"Well golly Gary, I can't help you with these! My magic is gnomish and is more focused on plants and trees! What if we get Morris, he's a helpful friend, to dig you a pit with a bottomless end?"

Gary agreed, and back to Gertie's they went. Good thing Morris and Fred were friends! Morris agreed, for he just had to see, exactly how many socks would make a bottomless pit necessary. Lo and behold, it was a huge number. Morris the Mole's squinty eyes were as wide as saucers!

Morris dug and he dug, then took a break, then dug more, until neither Gary or Fred could see him anymore. The pit was so deep, it was pitch black! Hopefully all the socks would fit into a hole like that. After a really long time Morris reappeared, he looked tired and dirty and there were rocks in his ears.

"Well, that's as deep as it goes. Throw the socks in!" All three of them heaved and shoved the pile within! The socks tumbled and rumbled and rolled into the hole, which had been a really great job done by Morris the Mole, and down, down, down they went without too much of a hassle. It was surprisingly easy, considering there were enough socks to fill a small castle!

"My deepest thanks to you Morris and Fred! The sock problem's over and so ends my dread! You are welcome here always, and I really must say, I didn't mind hanging around with a gnome all day."

Fred smiled wide, then laughed with a great roar! "Oh Gary, feel free to knock again anytime on my door! The tension between us was silly and old, we don't always have to do as we're told! Rotting tree, healthy tree, does it really matter?" After that day Gary the Gremlin and Fred the Gnome were friends forever after.

Story 5
Morris's Misadventure

Morris the Mole was asleep in his hole, and slumbering 'til nightfall was his goal. He softly snored, and he sweetly dreamed. In his mind's eye were dirt and rocks as far as could be seen. His paws paddled the air like a dog in a pool, with claws sharp and pointed; they were his digging tools.

With a snort and a snuffle, he got to his feet, his eyes were still closed, his dreams were still sweet. While dreaming of digging he did so in the waking world too; he was sleep digging, as moles sometimes do. He dug in his dream and he dug in his hole; and in no time at all a long tunnel was there to behold. It went on and on and on some more, as dirt became stone on the tunnel's floor. It went deeper and deeper and deeper again! Morris the Mole was sleep digging without end.

After many long hours, he came to a stop. He opened his eyes, and he froze in shock. This wasn't his hole! Where was he now? He looked at his claws, and they were all muddy and brown.

"Oh dear," Morris said with a shake of his head, "It appears that I've been sleep digging again."

Wherever he was it was darker than dark, he was in some sort of cavern that was barren and stark. He wandered along, looking for clues. His tunnel back home must be around here somewhere and he was determined to find it too! Good thing moles can see with no light, and it was lucky he saw nothing that'd give him a fright. Though all he saw were stalagmites and stalactites and a small pool of water. No sign of his tunnel, and it was starting to bother.

He looked to the right, and he looked to the left, he even tried looking up and he even tried looking down, but even then, his tunnel still could not be found. If he dug the wrong way, he'd never see Gertie's Garden again! To find the tunnel he had dug was the only way to get back to his friends. He scouted the cave, and it was quite empty, nothing of note except the puddle, there was no way in, no way out, not even a bat! Just stones and rocks and the melancholy dripping of water, which was beginning to be a bit of a bother. Drip, drip, drip, it made Morris so irate! Then it made him remember something! His paws were muddy, oh this was great! The only water around was in the small lake! Morris shook his head, he felt like such a fool! The way back up was by the small pool! He searched and he sniffed and lo and behold, he found the tunnel that would lead back to his hole. It had been behind a rock, nearly impossible to see, and finding it made Morris smile with glee! He scuttled inside, and after a long trek through the winding tunnel, sometimes feeling like he was being strained through a funnel, he found his way home and was rather surprised! Why Morris could scarcely believe his eyes! There were even more tunnels inside his hole!

"How much sleep digging did I do?" thought Morris the Mole. He simply shook his head and went back to bed, hoping this nonsense wouldn't happen again.

Story 6
Sydney Squeaks

The roar of thunder bellowed, the rain fell in sheets, but Fred and Morris were safely sheltered within the burrow under the tree. The booms and the bangs crashed down loudly in the cruel raging storm, it was really quite frightening, but at least Fred and Morris were safe inside where it was warm and inviting, away from all that thunder and lightning.

They were cozy and comfy and playing some games, when a knock at the entrance came through the loud whispers of rain. Fred got to his feet and he opened the door, and there stood dripping and drooping a creature out in the storm! She was furry and soggy and absolutely soaked! She'd be wanting a towel to dry off, Fred would hope! He recognized the creature as Sydney Squeaks, a squirrel who lived up in the boughs of his tree.

He ushered her in and after her fur was dried, Sydney Squeaks started to cry. She told Fred and Morris that her drey had been destroyed, by something had been impossible to avoid! It had fallen apart in the harsh driving rain, and to build a new one would be such a pain! She seemed so distraught that Fred resolved to help, and Morris was willing to lend aid as well. Though going about doing it might be a problem; Sydney lived up, up, up near the top of the tree, while Fred and Morris preferred to live underground, you see. A squirrel underground simply wouldn't do! Squirrels lived in trees and that was what she'd want to do too, but moles aren't tree climbers and gnomes don't like high places; they much prefer underground spaces.

Another issue that was plain to see, is that gnomes and moles don't know how to build in a tree. Squirrels like to use leaves and sticks to make their nests, whereas Morris and Fred thought stones were best. Differences aside, they'd try their utmost if it took all day, since they had promised Sydney Squeaks that they'd help rebuild her drey. After all, they were her only neighbours, and Sydney was always happy to give them favours. She'd helped Morris and Fred to store food in their homes, and she'd happily planted flowers with Fred the Gnome. She was their neighbour who helped in the garden and she deserved to have a happy home due to her help with guarding. She was as much a sentinel to Gertie's Garden as Morris or Fred; it was just that she liked to live in high places instead. They didn't quite know how to go about helping, but sometimes it's better to simply do something.

The next night when Gertie was asleep, all three critters emerged from under the tree. They decided that Morris would gather debris, and Fred would try to get up the tree. He took a running start, then he sprang into a leap! He got a good hold on the bark of the tree. He scooted and scuttled but couldn't quite get up, so he let himself drop with a soft little thump.

It was becoming clear Fred and Morris might not be much help here, but Sydney shouldn't be homeless and she didn't like their burrows. It was enough to cause all of their brows to furrow! If only there was some way to make a drey that had the strength of rock and couldn't be swept away. Fred thought for a moment, then had an idea! Gary Gremlin had showed him how to animate stone! Perhaps they could do the same with sticks and rebuild Sydney's home!

He went into his burrow and returned with a stick, he gave it a wave and he gave it a kick. "Nibbity, Nobbity, Sorcerous Gnome! Come alive you stick, and rebuild Sydney's home!"

Up the stick leapt, and wobbled up the tree. It wiggled and waggled; it was truly a sight to see. It settled between the space of two thick branches, and Sydney was impressed, as you could probably imagine. Fred did it again and again and again, happy he was able to help out his friend. In no time at all, the drey was rebuilt! It had a neat look, as if it were on stilts. The magical sticks looked normal to passersby, but truly there was so much more there than meets the eye. They were as strong as stone and could bend without breaking, they would sway with the wind and it was oh so breathtaking.

It may have taken a while to figure it out, but Sydney Squeaks was pleased with her new home, no doubt! The next time there was lightning, Sydney was fine! She was in her magical drey; cozy, warm and dry.

Story 7
The Ants' Missing Apples

The Queen of the Ants was wandering amongst the plants, watching in amusement as they swayed and they danced. The wind was pleasant, little more than a gust, carrying dandelion fluff with it like fine motes of dust. She was making her way from her nest to ants' tree; it had been enchanted by Fred to produce apples, you see. She got where she was going, and then looked around. There weren't any apples lying on the ground!

She chittered and chattered and issued commands. They'd have to take this issue up with the lord of the land! There was an agreement between Fred and the ants; the queen and her subjects would not eat the plants. Instead, they'd have apples, so when they found the tree bare, imagine their shock! No apples, no cores, not even a seed! Someone had picked clean the apple tree!

She gathered her subjects and onward they marched, Fred's burrow under the tree was their mark. They had to tell Fred, and had to do it soon! The plants of the garden looked so delicious in full bloom! They'd come to appreciate the beauty of it, but they still had to eat! It was either the leaves of the plants or the apples of the tree.

They arrived at Fred's door and they chittered and chattered. Fred soon came out to see what was the matter. It didn't take him too long to understand: there was no longer a functional apple tree on Gertie's land! He ran to the tree, and it was as he suspected. No apples, no cores, not even a seed! He'd have to fix this quick; the ants were in need!

He did a "Nibbity, Nobbity, Sorcerous Gnome!" yet there were still no apples to be found on the tree or in the loam. Not even gnome magic could make the tree bear fruit, though luckily Fred knew someone who'd know what to do!

A few minutes later, Gary the Gremlin was on the scene! With his knowledge of curses perhaps the cause of the blight could be gleaned, as no other alternative was easily seen.

"Have you gone "Nibbity, Nobbity, Sorcerous Gnome?" Gary asked as he poked around in the dark and wet loam.

"Indeed, I have, indeed I did, though nothing seemed to come of it," said Fred the Gnome, a little bit worried. Hopefully this problem would be solved if Gary hurried.

"The only one with knowledge of curses around here is me; it seems someone or something simply ate everything on the tree. They did it so fast and they did it so quick, that now the tree won't bear fruit because it's exhausted from it!"

Fred looked confused, then he had an idea! With a wave of his hand and a swish of his beard, upon the bark he made a face appear! Why waste time wondering when you could talk to the one who was there?

"Excuse me Mr. Tree, 'tis I Fred the Gnome. What can we do to get you to drop fresh apples once again to feed the ants that call this garden home?"

The tree swayed, then opened its mouth. It sounded rather morose as it gazed towards the house. "I'm sorry my friend, I would if I could, I have failed to bear fruit like an apple tree should. Though it's nothing sinister, there's nothing amiss, I simply need to rest for a bit. Though magic I be, even I have a limit, and I fear my friend that I have hit it. While you all slumbered, while you all slept, it was Gertie who discovered my fruit which over you fret! She picked it all to make pies for church and neighbours; really my friends, it was hers to take! How was she to know the need for apples would be so great? So, the next time she comes, do something to show how badly you all need the apples I grow."

The tree spoke the truth, so Fred returned to his burrow. If he worked quickly, he could have the solution ready by tomorrow! He Gnomed, then he Nibbitied, and then he Nobbitied, until finally he had a way to tell Gertie those apples were shared property. It was simply a glyph on a piece of bark, no different from the one used the time Gertie had left cookies in the yard.

He left it by the door as night turned to morn, and hoped that this problem would trouble them no more. As dawn turned to day, then in the late afternoon, Gertie emerged to plant a plant or two. She saw the enchanted bark, and was a bit surprised. She ran her finger over it, and something appeared before her eyes. A floating apple, so plump and so red, then it turned to nothing but a core instead. The core became a hand that pointed to the tree, where no more apples grew, it was plain to see. The tree was absolutely spent, and Gertie quickly understood what the glyph meant. She planted her plants, left a note for Fred, left something by the door, and then went to bed.

That night Fred awoke, hopeful it worked. He ran to the door and flung it open with a jerk. He ran to the backdoor, and nearly tripped on the note!

My apologies garden guardian, I didn't mean to offend. I was simply surprised to see so many apples on my land! I picked them to make pies for my friends and my church. If I had known how important they were to you I would have asked first! So, to say I'm sorry and put this problem to rest, I present you with not cookies this

time, but pies instead! Will two be enough? I left them by the door.
Let me know if you need some more.

Fred looked to the door, and there were the pies. They were absolutely gigantic in size! The ants would be fed for many, many days! Thank goodness that Gertie was so very great! The ants were fed, and Fred had pie too, as did Morris and Gary and Sydney Squeaks; by the looks of things here they'd all be fed for weeks! It took a few days for the tree to again bear fruit, and after it did Gertie always left at least one or two. She still made her pies, but made it a point to share; she always gave some to the critters in her garden, because Gertie cared.

Story 8
Fred's Cousin Nigel Feather Toes

It was an extra special occasion in Gertie's Garden today! Fred's cousin Nigel was coming to stay; it was such an occasion because he lived so far away. Not the next house over or out in the forest, no Nigel lived over the land and across the sea; Nigel lived in England, you see. "Now how does Nigel get to Canada from so far away?" I know that is something you'd be inclined to say. Well, you're right in thinking it isn't easy, especially since boats make Nigel queasy. No, instead, with the help of Fred and gnomish magic, Nigel made his way to Canada in a way that was rather outlandish! There was a fairy ring in the forest not far from Fred's tree, and that was how Nigel visited with relative ease. Every May the thirteenth at twenty-past-two, Fred had some gnomish magic to do. He'd uncork a potion and pour it on the ground, right in the centre of the circle that mushrooms grew around. Then he Nibbitied, he Nobbitied, he Sorcerous Gnomed! Just like that, Nigel would pop out of the loam! He'd be a bit dirty so he brought a spare set of clothes, but if you were wondering how Nigel got to Canada at least now you know.

"Why, hello there Fred, a hail and a hello and how do you do?" Nigel looked a lot like Fred, from the boots on his feet to the hat on his head, though there was the exception that his cap differed from Fred's; his was a nice shade of blue instead of bright red.

"Hello and greetings and welcome cousin! Fredrick Jerome Kopillus Gnome is happy to invite you to his cozy little home!"

So out of the forest and past the stream, the great leafy top of Fred's tree could be seen. They walked and they talked and they caught up on many things, until eventually the fence could be seen. It was dark as dark could be, because could you imagine? A gnome out in the daylight would give Gertie a fright! Better to escort Nigel under cover of night.

They got to the fence and Fred snuck through a gap, followed closely by Nigel with his hand on his cap. Then there they were, home sweet home, well I suppose home only for Fred the Gnome.

"Why, what a nice garden, I really must say, though I wonder what it would look like in the bright light of day?" Nigel furrowed his brow and surveyed the land. He'd only ever seen it at night, you understand.

"It looks much the same, though for wanting to see it in the daylight I cannot lay blame, it really is a shame it can only be viewed by us at night. If we were to do it at midday it'd give Gertie a fright."

"Perhaps one day, cousin," said Nigel as he continued to walk. They went back to Fred's burrow to talk.

While they went inside, Morris came out. He thought he heard voices in the garden speaking aloud. He looked over here and he looked over there, but he couldn't find the people who'd been talking anywhere. He sniffed around the shed, then he sniffed around the tree. He thought he smelled a new smell, but he didn't see how; Morris knew all the smells of the garden by now.

"Queen of the Ants have you seen anyone new?"

"Why no Morris I haven't, have you?"

"Sydney, oh Sydney high up in your drey, have you seen anyone new come to the garden today?"

"No Morris I haven't, but I cannot be certain. Perhaps Gary the Gremlin could locate the mystery person?"

Sydney and Morris made their way over to Gary's. The yard was quite barren and the residents quite scary. There were goo trails and slimy snails and bloodsuckers all over. A rather nasty shock considering it was right beside the garden of which Gertie was the owner.

They went to the rock pile under which Gary dwelled, trying to ignore the smells they smelled. He answered the door and ushered them in; if anyone could help them, it would be him. They would've gone to Fred but he'd been missing all day, so perhaps Gary the Gremlin would have something helpful to say.

"Hello neighbours, how do you do? What is it I can be doing for you?"

"I think there's someone new in the garden; I sniffed a new scent! On top of that nobody knows where Fred went." Morris looked rather anxious and Sydney a bit worried. Luckily Gary knew what to do in a hurry.

He picked up a rock, polished it well, then he began to cast a gremlin spell! "Skibbidy Skobbidy Sorcerous Gremlin!" And just like that the surface was much more reflective. It showed Fred the Gnome, safe in his home. But whoever was with him must've been the person unknown! He looked just like him, but had a blue hat. None of them would have ever imagined that!

"Does Fred have a twin?" Gary asks his stunned neighbours.

"Not that he's mentioned, though I guess we'll ask later."

Sydney perked up, and then she said, "Wait, could it just be Fred's cousin come to visit instead? I think I recall hearing Fred say that

Nigel Feather Toes comes to stay each and every year on the thirteenth of May."

The mystery was solved, and they all went to Fred's. Rather than investigate they came bearing presents instead! They got to meet Nigel and learned where Fred had been all day, and they had a good laugh over the lengths they had gone to when they could've just asked. Fred decided to inform his friends when Nigel Feather Toes would be visiting again; in return the others promised not to scry and to spy; next time they'd make sure to simply drop by. So that's how it was, and that's how it ends. Simply the story of one of the many times that Nigel visited Fred.

Story 9
Winter at Gertie's

The howl of the wind, the harsh chill of ice. Winter in Gertie's Garden wasn't always so nice. There wasn't much to look after; every tree and plant was bare. Though at least it wasn't lonely, since nobody hibernated there. Sure, the ants hunkered down far underground, to the point that by only Morris could they be found. Sydney was around, as was Fred. Even Morris liked to get out from under his shed. Winter at Gertie's was just getting started, and that meant leisure time for the critters in her garden.

Sydney stored food, enough for all three, and often they found themselves all cozy under the tree. Fred's burrow was warm, Sydney's drey a bit cold. As for Morris, well, he lived in a hole. Most days during the winter they played games and they talked, sometimes for fun Fred would attempt to enchant a rock. Sydney might try to make a new recipe with her stored food, and Morris tried to expand both his hole and Fred's burrow, too. They couldn't really go out, but that was okay. Inside was where they were, and it's where they would stay.

They cooked and they cleaned and they had fun playing games, though without the greenery of the garden it just wasn't the same. They became bored after just a week or two, though luckily Morris knew just what to do!

"Sydney and Fred, Fred and Sydney, would you like to go on an adventure with me? One time in the past I sleep dug into a cave! Maybe we could find another one if we're feeling brave."

Sydney squeaked in protest! She was a tree squirrel, not a ground squirrel! Being so far underground was enough to make her tail curl! After a bit of thinking, she decided to try, but she had reservations and Morris would have to hear why!

"Squeak I say!" said Sydney with a twitch of her nose, "We squirrels don't belong underground you know! I'm hesitant but bored, and I need an adventure! I suppose I'll give it a try; I hope it brings pleasure."

Now Fred was quite used to underground spaces, it's just his burrow was under a tree and not deep underground, which wasn't exactly a place where gnomes were normally found. "Morris, my mole, my friend and my neighbour, is there some way we can do this that's safer? Maybe supports? Perhaps a map or a guide? What do we do if we get trapped inside?"

Normally Morris would think and then answer, but being stuck inside for so long was such a damper! He needed something new, and he needed it quick! Morris, normally patient, wouldn't listen to it!

"Friends, friends, no need to worry! It's safe and it's fine. Now come along, tunneling is divine!" and so off they went to the home of Morris the Mole, where Morris chose a spot to start digging a hole. He dug, and he dug, and he dug deep, deep down. He didn't notice Sydney's fearful eyes or Fred's grumpy frown. No supports, no helmets, not even a light! What made Morris think that this was alright?

Deeper and deeper, down, down, down they went; Morris was tired, his energy spent. They burst into a cave, and he slumped over panting. Who knew tunneling could be so demanding? The ground was frozen solid; this was much more exerting than summer digging or garden working. Wherever they were it was dark as could be, but Fred got the sense they were under his tree. Deep, deep down past the roots and into the stone, but still he was certain they were under his home.

"Squeak!" said Sydney, looking around, "Exactly how far are we underground?"

"I have no idea," remarked Fred, though in his heart he felt a pang of dread.

Morris was tired and almost asleep, though luckily Fred had a trick up his sleeve. "Nibbity, Nobbity, Sorcerous Gnome! Let there be light to find my way home!" and so there was light that shone through the cave, and it seemed to branch off two different ways. One was a dark tunnel, serpentine and winding, the other was half-flooded with water, which was something worth minding.

Sydney sniffed over here, and then over there, and to her the choice quickly became clear, "We should go in the dark tunnel; I smell something neat! I think it might be something good to eat! The flooded tunnel seems to be a dead end, though I suppose I'll hear what you have to say, Fred."

Fred thought for a moment, then decided water was work. Who even knew what within it would lurk? Better to eat food than to become it, plus there was a rumbling in his gnomish stomach, "I support your decision and we'll go that way! Untold snacks shall be ours this day!"

So off they went with Morris in tow, though he was half-asleep just so you know, deep into the dark, they were ever so brave, though keep in mind Fred was still illuminating the cave. They went this way, that way, and a bit to the left, and finally what they had found became clear to Fred. It wasn't food at all, but a fairy ring! What a wonderful, magical, beautiful thing!

"Squeak!" said Sydney, a little surprised, "What's this nonsense before my eyes? This isn't food, this is just fungus! I was rather hoping there would be some food among us!"

"Sydney," Fred remarked, "I think I found our way out! Morris is too tired, that's without a doubt."

They glanced over to Morris, who was sleeping and still, and so they turned back to the mushrooms on the little hill. "We can use this fairy ring to get back to the tree! Then we can eat food and then go to sleep! We'll still have the tunnel so we can always come back, maybe the flooded one would be good for a laugh."

Sydney nodded in agreement with a cordial "Squeak!" and so Fred began to speak:

"Nibbity, Nobbity, Sorcerous Gnome! Fairy ring please guide me and my friends back to our under-tree home!"

With a flash, and a pop, and a bright, bright light, they ended up back in Fred's home and everything was alright. Morris awoke as Sydney went off to find something to eat, and he rubbed his eyes as he looked around the burrow under the tree.

"My apologies Fred, I've been a fool. I shouldn't have dragged you all caving without any tools! I just wanted us all to have an adventure together, and instead fell asleep in the Earth's frozen nethers."

Fred smiled widely as he spoke, "That's okay Morris, we still had fun, no joke! We found a fairy ring and it beat sitting inside, though perhaps we could have our voices heard more next time."

Before he could respond Sydney came back with food, and not long after the under-tree burrow was full of dozing critters all in a good mood.

Story 10
A Night Off

It was a beautiful evening in Gertie's backyard, the air was warm and the sun had just set, though it was more like twilight rather than night yet. The flowers were pristine, the lawn was watered, the plants were planted and not a weed in sight, it looked like Fred wouldn't have much to do this night! Perhaps he'd visit Morris, that sounded alright.

Morris popped out of his hole before Fred could say "Hi", he would've asked why Fred was there but he already knew why. They were the garden guardians and the lords of the land, but how were they to tend a garden that was already well in hand?

"Here to hang-out because there's nothing to tend? Alright Fred, maybe it'd be a nice night to hang out with friends. Perhaps Sydney or Gary or the ants would like to come along? The more the merrier and we haven't a night off in so long."

Fred nodded in agreement and then off they went, first they got Sydney who looked bored by some flowers, though the ants informed them they worked through the nighttime hours. Gary was happy to have something to do, since gremlins were rather social and liked novelty too.

So, the four all gathered in Gertie's Garden, and it was about time the fun got started. What would they do? Where would they go? The one caveat here was that nobody knows!

"We could go spelunking."

"We could explore in the trees!"

"We could go to my burrow and play games peacefully!"

Everyone had ideas, but nobody agreed. That was until Gary spoke up, you see, "Friends, what if we went into the forest just past the fence? Bickering here will just make us all tense. What we really need is something brand new! Maybe we'll even meet people in the forest too!"

It sounded like fun, and it was the best idea they had, and to everyone there it didn't sound half bad! Over the fence they went -

except of course for Morris who preferred digging and went under instead - into the forest past the land of Fred! The trees were dense but they framed a nice pond, and the four friends were ready to explore the wilds beyond.

"Well, here we are, out in the woods. From what I've heard there's fun to be had in this neighbourhood." Gary Gremlin looked to the right, and then he looked to the left, and he smiled thinking of the fun he'd have tonight with his friends.

Sydney sniffed around and so did Morris, though Fred simply wondered what to do next. He wanted an adventure that would excite his friends. Perhaps they'd find fairies if any were out, though they were bound to find something out here, that was no doubt.

They wandered to the east, then to the west, then they were all in agreement going south was best. They wandered a bit, then found themselves lost. Nothing to worry about, they all decided, simply find a fairy ring and step inside it. Fred could use it to get everyone home! That was a handy trick that could only be performed by a gnome. They passed a big bear going the other way, but he didn't feel talkative and had nothing to say. The birds chirped overhead but didn't quite carry a tune. The friends began to hope they'd make it home soon.

The darker it got the more lost they became, and the more the forest seemed less than tame. There were hoots and howls and the snapping of twigs, and something that sounded vaguely like a pig. Whatever it was and wherever they were, the fear inside them began to stir.

"We need to go home!" moaned Morris the Mole, who'd very much prefer to be back in his hole.

"Squeak!" said Sydney, chilled to the bone. She too would prefer to be back home.

Gary was quiet, but his gaze shifted quite a bit, and Fred had certainly had enough of this. If only there was something to guide them, to show and to lead! Then Fred thought a thought he could scarcely believe! He saw a mushroom, much like the ones from the ring, and another like it further away, it was the darndest thing! With little recourse and no ideas left, he decided he and his friends would get home yet!

The shriek of an owl with outstretched talons sent all four scurrying towards the mushrooms, nearly losing their balance! They scuttled and hurried and sprinted and scurried and luckily, after running a bit, they found the way back and they were so happy to see it. The fairy ring sat in a clearing a bit far away, thanks to the mushrooms that had shown them the way! They ran over and stepped in as Fred said the words: "Nibbity, Nobbity, Sorcerous Gnome! Fairy ring guide me and my friends back home!"

With a whoosh and a swoosh and a bright, bright light, they found themselves back and all was alright! Well, all except one thing, a minor thing really. They were back in the caverns underneath the tree instead of the burrow as intended, you see. Fred was confused, but then he remembered! They could still all have some fun times together!

"The tunnel that's flooded we never explored, that's something we've never done before!"

Gary perked up; he had something to add! "Gremlins have a spell to let you breathe underwater, so that wouldn't be half bad!" The others agreed, and off they went. They still had most of a night off and now knew how it would be spent!

They explored and they swam and they spelunked the rest of the time, finally parting ways at the end of the night. It was close to dawn, but they didn't mind. A good adventure was hard to find. They all went home and went to sleep, a wonderful time that was capped off by counting sheep.

Book 2: Nathan the Knight

Part 1

Nathan the Knight was decked out in his shiny plate armour, his trusty sword sheathed at his side and his equally trusty shield strapped to his back. Looking at himself in the gilded mirror, his blonde hair hung a bit limply, and he was young enough to look somewhere between a teenager and an adult. He was excited because today was the day that he was going to be made an initiate of the Knights of the Order and leave on his quest! His family had sent their oldest son to be a courageous and valiant knight for the kingdom for as long as anyone could remember. He was the eldest of this generation, and here he was preparing to see the king, ready to accept his noble quest! Then he would be a full-fledged Knight of the Order, and he'd live happily ever after fighting evil and upholding his beliefs.

He felt very nervous though. He was going to be far away from home for the first time, his family was putting a lot of pressure on him, and he had to please the king, too! He had been a squire yesterday, but now he was wearing armour and charging out into the countryside to fight evil? Seemed a bit premature to Nathan.

He took one final look in the mirror. He was sort of tall, and the armour looked really intricate with its embossed details and chiseled emblems. He felt somewhat out of place wearing it though, like he hadn't earned it yet. Like it was a costume. That thought didn't linger long though; it was abruptly cut off by a loud knocking on the door to his chambers.

"Nathan? Are you prepared for your journey?" came the voice of his valet, Tyrus. He was a wise old man who'd seen countless members of Nathan's family off on their quests before. He poked his head into the room; his smile was one of reassurance, but it didn't do much to dispel the bundle of nerves in Nathan's stomach.

"Yes. I'm prepared." He certainly didn't feel that way, but he had a duty to uphold. Nathan somewhat clumsily exited the room, still getting used to how heavy and restrictive plate mail was. He creaked as he moved and every step was awkward and heavy. How was he supposed to fight evil in this armour? He could barely walk in it!

Nathan had to use the wall to keep upright causing his cumbersome spaulders to scrape against the hard stone, eliciting an unpleasant screech. This was going to be a difficult journey.

"Master Nathan, are you still with us?" came the voice of Tyrus from down the hall.

Nathan nearly tore a tapestry off the wall as he stumbled around a pillar. "Yes! I'm coming, just having a bit of a mobility issue!" He clanged and creaked loudly doing so, but he managed to stand on his own two feet. His plate greaves were horribly stiff and restrictive, but you couldn't fight evil in your stockings. Or could you?

Nathan clumsily and stiffly clambered down the stone hallway, turned left, and came face-to-face with his first real adversary. Stairs. Specifically, a spiral staircase. He needed to get to the great hall, but he could barely manage to walk down a hallway let alone descend the eastern turret. He flattened himself as best he could against the wall of the tower, and slowly side-stepped each stair. One, two, one, two. Nathan managed to get down the flight without much trouble, though it took him a long time.

By the time he had fully descended the seemingly endless staircase, he finally arrived on the first floor of the family castle, and was beginning to get the hang of moving in plate mail. He still creaked and felt a bit clumsy, but at least he could walk without too many problems now. Now that he could walk, evil would fall before him!

"Nathan, are you prepared to take your vows?" the sound of Tyrus' voice made Nathan jump, and he whirled around awkwardly to face the aging valet.

"Yes, of course. Lead on, Tyrus, I'm ready to become a full-fledged knight in service to the king." Nathan really hoped his apprehension at this grand duty wasn't obvious.

Tyrus lifted a bushy white eyebrow, but didn't mention whatever it was he felt he needed to raise an eyebrow at. "Yes, well, follow on."

A short walk down the hall, adorned with torches and tapestries and stained-glass windows, got them where they were headed. The huge oaken doors of the great hall stood open before them, and the braziers were lit with bright fire to illuminate the colossal feast hall.

Armoured knights, nobility, Nathan's family and even the king himself were all assembled along the sides of the room, seated at long tables, and all their collective eyes fell upon him as he entered. Nathan shifted nervously under their gaze, and felt himself sweat a little. He felt not just their eyes on him, but also their expectations, their envy and their judgement. Would he be able to go through with this?

The commanding voice of the announcer rang out suddenly, startling Nathan a bit, "All rise for the initiate of the Knight's Order! Nathan of the noble house of Havarshire hath been nominated for a quest of greatest import to prove himself worthy of being a full member of the King's Knights. He hath arrived, and lo it is time for the king himself to personally assign the quest to the initiate!"

The king was seated at the end of the hallway, looking intimidating despite his reputation for kindness. Nathan was finding it a bit hard to breathe. He took a shaky step forward, then another, and let his legs guide him towards His Majesty, seemingly of their own accord. He wished he was wearing a helmet with which to mask his nervousness, but still managed to stop before the table and awkwardly get down on one knee before the sovereign.

"I-I'm here, Y-Your Majesty," Nathan said, mortified at his mumbled and stuttered greeting. Nobody seemed to notice, but Nathan certainly did.

The king rose and walked around to Nathan as he began speaking, his dark blue robes trailing behind him as he did, "Ah yes, Nathan Havarshire! Your family has served the kingdom loyally for many generations, and it is my honour to bestow upon you the quest that will make you a full-fledged Knight of the Order!"

Nathan was shaking in his plate mail. He wasn't sure he could do this. The king was right in front of him now, and he'd be able to see the doubt and worry on his face. His Majesty paused momentarily, looked upon Nathan's worried countenance, and whispered discretely, "Worry not young one, thine victory is assured. Believe in thyself as I do."

Nathan's resolve was bolstered by the kind comment, and the king tried to speak a little more than necessary to allow Nathan time to collect himself. One of the perks of being the king was you could drone on about any old thing and everyone would be spellbound.

"We are gathered here today to mark this day of grand importance! A malevolent force hath taken residence in the neighbouring kingdom of Kyrbor, the king of which we have called a staunch ally for many seasons. Nathan Havarshire shall ride to this allied kingdom and aid the king in diffusing the situation! Wherever there be evil in that land, it shall be expunged!" The king glanced at Nathan, decided he could use a little longer to strengthen his nerve, and continued speaking, "We know not the nature of the disturbance, just that the kingdom has asked us for aid, and we shall swiftly deliver it!"

"So sayeth the king, so shall it be done!" was loudly chanted throughout the great hall of Castle Havarshire, echoing and resounding throughout both the room and Nathan's head. It was still overwhelming, but he knew what he had to do. The king believed in him as did his family, and he himself believed in upholding the tradition of serving the crown. He would not fail.

The king allowed the room to chant and cheer for a while, and finally decided to silence them with a wave of his hand when he noticed Nathan looked determined rather than frightened. "Loyal subjects, the time has come to see our new initiate off! He rides to Kyrbor this day!"

Many cheers again erupted, and at long last the king tapped a sword on both of Nathan's spaulders. A symbolic gesture, but still one that filled Nathan with pride. It meant he was a probationary Knight of the Order, and would become a full-fledged one upon completing his quest. The knotted ball of nerves in his stomach mercifully unravelled, his heart now filled with purpose rather than dread.

"I shall serve thee unfailing, Your Majesty," Nathan said as he rose to his feet again. His leg was a little stiff from being down on one knee for so long. He resisted the urge to shake his somewhat asleep leg though; Nathan thought it wouldn't look very knightly of him to do a weird dance in the great hall.

"I have complete faith you will, young one," the king said as he nodded at Nathan, a signal to march from the great hall to the stables to tack-up a war steed and ride off to one's quest, as was tradition. Nathan saluted and marched with renewed purpose out of the great hall, still slightly nervous but now more determined than afraid. He believed in himself as the king did.

He strode with purpose, no longer feeling quite as clumsy in his shining plate mail. He wasn't unsure or afraid. He was ready. Nathan made his way to the stables, his new war steed already tacked and awaiting him. One of the seemingly endless rituals that was a part of the initiation was gifting a war horse to the initiate. He was expected to name it according to some defining moment during the quest. He mounted the horse, somewhat clumsily but he managed, and it followed his commands as he squeezed his calves together to get it to walk forward.

"Best of luck, my lord!" said the stableboy, a wide smile on his dirty face. Nathan reciprocated the smile, waving as he rode off. He was going to fight so much evil.

Part 2

Luckily for Nathan, he left the castle mid-morning and Kyrbor was only a couple hours away by horseback. He'd be there by the day's end, and he wouldn't have to make camp on the way. Which was fortunate, because he wasn't really sure how to make camp with a horse. His journey through the countryside was fairly quiet; he mostly just rode through small hamlets and over dirt roads on the way out of his own kingdom. He passed through vibrant forests of trees and flowers, plains dotted with infrequent oak trees and small lakes, by beautiful churches made of wooden planks and stained glass with impressive steeples, and farmhouses with thatched roofs and somewhat uneven cobblestone walls. It was a pastoral and scenic ride to Kyrbor, one where Nathan was mostly alone with his thoughts.

Those thoughts were focused on the nature of the evil he'd be facing, like what it even was. Nobody had given him much in the way of details, so he could be doing something as grand and heroic as slaying a dragon or as mundane as arbitrating a trade dispute between local merchant guilds. The uncertainty wasn't great for relieving his nerves, but with the belief and favour of the king behind him, Nathan didn't feel like there was anything he couldn't overcome. He daydreamed of slaying dragons and fighting rampaging ogres, of using diplomacy to quell wars and disputes, and of being welcomed into the Order with open arms.

He barely noticed when he passed into Kyrbor; it was only an old wooden sign by the road declaring one was entering it anyway. The sun was directly overhead in such a way that Nathan was fairly certain it was a little past noon. He decided to stop, both to feed himself and his steed. He hadn't really bonded with the nameless horse much, though he had a burgeoning fondness for it. It was basically his partner in fighting evil, and in the Order a knight's horse was held in nearly as high esteem as the rest of its members.

He made the horse slowdown from its walking pace, dismounted somewhat clumsily, and tied it to a nearby oak tree. Nathan dug into one of the brown leather saddle bags and produced some wheat, which he then proceeded to feed to his horse. It lazily chewed the offering.

"I guess we're a team. I don't know what to call you, but I'm starting to like you," Nathan said as he stroked the horse's mane. It bobbed its head in response. The horse had a happy look in its eyes and seemed to enjoy Nathan feeding it and petting it, which was good, because Nathan wasn't sure how fighting evil would work with an unruly steed. The Order was insistent that a team was only as strong as its cohesiveness, and that infighting was a greater threat to peace and order than any outside force.

Once his still nameless horse had eaten and been led to a nearby stream, Nathan ate bread and drank water from a wineskin, looking out across the plains. It was beautiful out there, and it had been some time since Nathan had ventured outside his family's estate. The fields of vibrant green plants low to the ground with the occasional tall stalk poking through stretched as far as he could see on his right, with some shrubs and trees beside a river that bordered a forest to his left. It put him at ease to be out here, and he allowed himself to relax, at least until he was finished eating.

After taking in the scenery one last time, Nathan untied his horse from the tree by the stream, mounted, and rode off down the road, still with farmland on one side and forest on the other, as he began the rest of the journey towards Kyrbor's capital. It was now only a few hours to the king of Kyrbor's castle.

After some time, Nathan was riding on a dirt road through a dense forest. Both he and his horse were startled by a panicked cry for help that cut through the air. Quickly looking around, he saw a wagon with a broken wheel just off the road, with two men in black hoods and studded leather brandishing daggers, one holding hostage a frightened merchant and the other inspecting crates on the broken wagon. The horse pulling the wagon was spooked, but didn't seem to be able to move with the wheel broken. It pulled on its harness, but seemed to be stuck.

Nathan hastily leapt off his horse, quickly tying it to a nearby tree as he crept through the brush to get a closer look. His hand hovered over his sword's hilt, and he was nervous but resolute. Somebody had to do something, and Knights of the Order were men of action! He tried to get the shield off his back, but fumbled and dropped it loudly.

"Oy! We've got another sneak trying to poach our mark!" The hooded men looked around, and Nathan knew he'd be spotted. He decided to reveal himself and demand they leave at once.

"Halt! Leave that merchant be, you blackguards!" Nathan hoped he sounded intimidating because he was kind of scared, "Leave this wood, or by the authority of the king I shall have you in chains!"

The hooded men didn't speak, they just attacked. Nathan had never been in a true fight before; he had only sparred. There were some trees between them, so Nathan ducked behind one and stuck out his shield just as one of the bandits charged past. He hit the shield headfirst with a clang and dropped to the ground with a loud thud, his body landing in a bed of leaves and twigs and his blade falling out of his hand. He groaned, but was clearly no longer a threat.

The crunching of leaves and twigs stopped abruptly, and Nathan couldn't see where the other one had gone. He peered cautiously around the tree, but saw nothing.

"My Lord, he's behind you!" called the merchant, eyes as wide as saucers. Nathan whirled around, his shield in front of his chest and his sword raised high. The bandit struck the centre of the shield, his blade loudly breaking as it scratched the surface of the gleaming shield with a loud screech and crumbled into shards at Nathan's feet. Taking advantage of the situation, Nathan brought his pommel down hard on the side of the bandit's head, knocking him out immediately. He collapsed, but Nathan was quick enough to catch his limp body with his shield arm and set the bandit down gently.

After checking on the merchant, who he learned was named Nyland, and tying up the bandits, Nathan and Nyland repaired the wagon as best they could. Since they were both headed to Castle Kyrbor, they rode off together. The bandits would face justice and nobody had been killed, which Nathan was happy about. Sometimes the Order was much too heavy-handed and was too focused on fixing the problem rather than the methods used to fix it. Why slay a dragon if you could just talk to it? The bandits probably weren't too pleased about it, but their hoods obscured most of their faces so it was hard to tell what they were feeling.

A breeze rolled over them as they left the dense forest behind and entered grasslands again. What few trees dotted the landscape had their leaves sighing in the wind, and the tall grass leaned in the breeze. All was green grass and blue skies and beautiful scenery as far as the eye could see, and it was peaceful.

Nathan looked over to Nyland, who seemed rather serious as he rode on his trading wagon. His ruffled coat and fine trousers looked somewhat out of place on a slightly aged and balding man, more appropriate for a youthful minstrel perhaps than a middle-aged merchant. Still, colourful dress likely complimented a colourful personality, and Nathan was feeling talkative.

"So, Nyland, from where do you hail?" Nathan glanced at the hard-packed dirt road ahead quickly so he didn't steer his still nameless horse into a stream, then looked back to the dour merchant.

Nyland jumped a bit, with Nathan getting the sense he had startled him from his thoughts. He looked to him for a moment, and just before it would have become uncomfortable, he began to speak in a somewhat quiet tone, "I hail from the far west, by the coast. As a young man I moved to Kyrbor to start a family and become a merchant rather than be a fisherman like the other men in my family. I was visiting my homeland for a time, then travelling to collect items to sell, and I was on my way back to Kyrbor when I was waylaid by bandits. Oddly enough they seem familiar..." his voice trailed off as he stared ahead. Nathan thought he seemed odd, but maybe he'd be more forthcoming later. Nathan was also sure to make a mental note about Nyland's comment on the bandits.

Nathan decided a lively conversation was likely not on the agenda today and decided to instead take in the scenery around him. The plains were beginning to give way to farmland, and it was certain Castle Kyrbor was nearby. Golden fields of wheat began to stretch further and further on either side, and farmhouses and homesteads began to dot the land beside the road. The occasional animal sound broke the silence, as did the sounds of farmers talking to their farmhands.

Just as Castle Kyrbor began to loom on the horizon, with its stout walls and tall towers seeming to scrape the clouds, frantic shouting pierced the formerly peaceful pastoral scene. Nathan looked around, and quickly saw what the cause of the commotion was near a barn a little off the road. A pack of wild dogs were fighting a group of farmers, and from the looks of it, the farmers were having a rough time. Nathan quickly charged his horse over, leapt off, tied it to a nearby fence in a hurry, and charged into the fray, unsheathing his sword and clumsily pulling his slightly scratched shield off his back as he did.

His appearance seemed to startle the dogs, and some shied away or fled. Nathan noticed some of them were rabid, and decided to focus on attacking those ones. Unlike the bandits, he saw no way to not kill in this situation. He didn't like it, but he'd have to actually take lives to save lives. He swung wide with his sword, hearing a pained yelp and a thud. Nathan felt ill, but he had to protect the farmers, and you couldn't reason with rabid animals. Another one snarled and lunged at him, got on top of his shield, clawed frantically, and fell to the ground. Nathan quickly plunged his sword into it, taking no pleasure in doing so. He thought he was going to be sick. The farmers were still shouting and attacking the dogs with pitch forks, and combat was proving a bit overwhelming for Nathan; not in a physical sense, but rather a psychological one.

He whirled around, panicked and terrified, ready to reluctantly slay the next dog. The farmers seemed to have it well in hand now, and Nathan was confident they'd be victorious and only suffer some minor injuries. What really grabbed his attention was a huge mange-ridden dog that had cornered a child a small distance away. The boy couldn't have been older than five, and he looked to be paralyzed with fear. The dog had its teeth bared, and almost seemed to savour the situation. Nathan sensed malevolence in that dog.

He charged at it without thinking, knocking a dog out of his way and eliciting a surprised yelp from it as he did, as he bellowed loudly and kept rushing at his target without breaking stride. The huge dog, which had matted brown fur and was the size of a large wolf, turned to look at Nathan with evil yellow eyes. No longer interested in the boy, it almost looked as if it was thinking as Nathan drew ever closer.

Just as Nathan was about to strike it, the dog jumped out of the way, then turned deftly and leapt onto Nathan's back, taking him to the ground with a noisy crash. His armour somewhat broke his fall, but it knocked the wind out of him. The combined weight of the armour and the dog made it hard to breathe. Rather than attack him though, the dog sat down on his back instead. It howled victoriously, a vile and dreadful bay full of sadistic joy, clearly enjoying watching Nathan suffer. The farmers were too busy with the other dogs to help him; his lungs quickly began to burn and he felt dizzy. It was getting harder to breathe, only coming in shallow pants now. Nathan was gripped by terror. Would this be the end of him?

His vision began to blur as he felt the weight become heavier and heavier upon him. He let himself go limp and accepted defeat, and by extension, the death that would soon accompany it. The shouts of the farmers and the yips and growls of the dogs sounded so distant now, with only the evil sounding growls of the dog to break up the sounds of combat. Without warning, a loud whinny broke out causing the dogs to yelp in surprise. The dog on Nathan shifted its weight slightly, seemingly to turn to look at something. The ground quaked, and with a deep growl of anger and surprise, the weight on Nathan was gone instantly! He was close to passing out, but he thought he heard the farmers cheer victoriously as the dog that nearly killed him growled and barked, then abruptly fell silent. Nathan heard a familiar neigh as he lost consciousness.

* * * * *

Nathan awoke somewhat hazy; he felt a little weak and short of breath, but otherwise okay. He tried to get up, immediately felt a shooting pain in his back, and stopped abruptly, a bit stunned. It was probably just a bruise, albeit a particularly nasty one. He glanced around as best he could while lying down. It seemed that he was in a farmhouse. There was a stone hearth with a warm fire crackling inside, a scratched wooden table flanked by similarly scratched benches, with a variety of bowls and tubs filled with vegetables haphazardly strewn about.

"You're lucky to be alive, you know," came a somewhat scolding voice from outside Nathan's field of view. It sounded like Nyland. "After that dog nearly killed you, the farmers sent someone to fetch a healer from Kyrbor. Your horse was actually the one to save you; it yanked on its rope until it snapped, then leapt at that dog like nothing I've ever seen before. He was your saving grace in that situation, I suppose. A loyal steed, isn't he? Smart, too. I tied him up outside, he seems content to wait for his master to return." Nathan still couldn't see who was speaking, but he was certain now it was Nyland. This informative monologue seemed like something he would do.

"Anyway, fortune favours you since you're still breathing. I'm glad to see you alive, though when we sent for a healer the farmers were going to ask for a high priest to raise you. Luckily, you'll just need some basic healing and you should be good to resume your journey to Kyrbor." As he finished speaking, Nyland came around to Nathan's bedside and stood there, looking around a bit.

"I almost died? Are the farmers okay at least? What of the child I ran to save?" Nathan's thoughts were still consumed by thoughts of the skirmish, as if it had never stopped. "Everyone is unharmed?"

Nyland nodded, smiling as he did. "You may have recklessly charged into a pack of wild animals, but it is lucky for those farmers you did. Outside of a couple minor cuts and scrapes, they're unharmed. The child was a bit shaken up but he was playing happily last I saw him so he'll probably be fine. You, however, almost got killed by that evil beast. I am certain that thing was no ordinary dog. Before you ask why I didn't join the fray, the only weapon I had was a crossbow and I obviously couldn't open fire with that onto a mixed field." Nyland examined a bowl by the bedside, then replaced it as he continued, "At any rate you seem to be doing your Order proud."

Nathan smiled at the kind words, though he was a bit confused, "You're much more talkative now than before. Why the change of heart? Last we spoke you were quite reserved."

Nyland shrugged, "I suppose it's because to aid a merchant is to invite the possibility of a reward. To aid peasants with little or nothing to give by charging head-long into combat for no reason other than the welfare of others was proof to me you weren't simply pretending. You truly are the proper type to be a Knight of the Order."

Nathan wasn't sure what to say, though luckily it was at this time the high priest arrived. He seemed happy to not have to raise anyone today, as it was apparently quite the ritual, but was more than happy to heal Nathan with his holy magic. He, too, was a member of the Knight's Order, specifically the Kyrbor Chapter, and was happy to aid an acolyte. Nathan felt much better after having his injuries healed by the priest, relatively minor though they were. It was more the shock of nearly dying and suffering defeat that bothered him. Curative magics couldn't just undo the fact that he now knew he wasn't invincible. Arresting the bandits had been so easy, how had he nearly died after getting outsmarted by a dog, of all things? He was proud he had been willing to charge into combat unthinkingly to save a child, though. It was proof he truly was a worthy member of the Order to so selflessly put a child's safety before his own as Nyland had pointed out. Nathan had upheld the tenets of the Order, and for that he could be proud; though thinking a little more next time before charging into combat was probably a good idea.

Nevertheless, Nathan had a mission to see to. He got himself out of bed and got back into his plate mail with help from Nyland, thanked the farmer who's house he had been carried into, and departed for Kyrbor along with Nyland and the high priest.

Part 3

Castle Kyrbor loomed before Nathan. The sight of it was formidable yet comforting; Nathan doubted he'd be accosted by dogs or bandits here, but being before the king would be nerve-wracking. The high priest had shown them the way and told them all matters of law were handled by the king himself, and as such the bandits were to be taken before him. The bandits were obviously not pleased about the matter, but hadn't made any attempts to escape either. They were still bound in Nyland's wagon.

Nathan absentmindedly stroked the mane of his steed; he had decided to name it "Saving Grace" both because of its timely rescue of him back with the dogs and also due to Nyland bringing it up in the farmhouse. Indeed, the saving grace of nearly dying was knowing his horse was indeed a fine war steed, and it finally had a proper name. Nathan could charge into combat with no reservations, but being in attendance at court always made him anxious somehow.

"We can't just stare at it; we'll have to enter at some point," remarked Nyland from the driver's seat of his wagon, "They'll need my testimony for the trial of the bandits and they'll need you to appear to receive your mission. After that, you'll need your armour repaired and I'll need my wagon looked at. Luckily, I know of a smith around here who happens to be beside a cartwright's shop, so we can get both of our issues resolved together. I figure you'll be wanting a guide around town, yes?" Nyland leaned out a bit to look at Nathan. He looked a lot livelier than he did previously, and his bardic ensemble was beginning to really suit him despite his age. Nathan nodded slowly. He was still nervous but at least he'd have the merchant he rescued by his side. Better to have company than to go it alone. Nathan dismounted Saving Grace, walking up to the halberdiers guarding the entrance nervously as he introduced himself.

* * * * *

The castle itself was a bit smaller than the estate of Nathan's family, which he found surprising. Sure, Kyrbor was a small kingdom, but it seemed odd for a noble family to have a residence grander than that of a king. It was richly adorned with red and blue tapestries and marble pillars though, so the décor made up for the relatively small size, at least in Nathan's eyes.

The great hall was a short walk through the castle, with the halberdiers escorting Nathan and Nyland along with the captured bandits. The bandits had been oddly quiet the entire time they had been captured, and Nathan had assumed it was because they were angry, but he was beginning to think it may be something else. Shame, maybe?

The thought dismissed itself as Nathan gazed into the great hall as the halberdiers opened the large wooden doors to reveal a series of stone hearths and tables with benches. At the end of the hall were more halberdiers, as the king seemed to be rather fond of them, and the king himself, seated behind a long table on a somewhat plain throne. The king had grey hair and dressed in dark colours, making him appear serious and a bit old. His face was creased a little by age but seemingly much more by worry. He didn't notice them enter the room until they were right in front of him; the king was sifting through letters and was very obviously preoccupied.

"Sire, the initiate of the Knight's Order has arrived. Nathan Havarshire stands before you, as does the merchant Nyland and two men captured and accused of banditry," said one of the halberdiers accompanying the group. He sounded a bit worried as he spoke, likely for the king's well-being. The king looked really overwhelmed by something in those letters.

The king looked up at them, seeming confused for a moment, though his confusion turned to joy as he broke into a wide and welcoming smile. "Ah! Young Nathan! Hello, hello! Your services are very much required in this most dire matter! You see, for months now, we've been plagued by attacks from wild animals. Now, normally that would be trivial, but it seems as if someone or something has been forcing them from the forest. The animals are often rabid and half-starved, leading me to believe some malevolent force is letting them loose on us purposefully. There used to be a tribe of orcs around here that would hunt in the forest, and they're the only thing

I could think of that would be causing this. We cannot lead an army into the forest against them, as they have unknown numbers and may be innocent." The king got to his feet and walked over to a window, then continued, "Obviously, we cannot attack without justification, though I am certain if the orcs aren't behind it, then they know who or what is. The forest I speak of is a few miles from the castle, and I believe since the orcs are known to still occasionally make their camp there, it's a good place to start."

The king raised a heavily ringed finger and pointed at a small mountain poking out of a dense sea of green. "There. That mountain holds the answer we seek, I know it. I, and by extension, your king and your Order, entrust you with seeking out the evil we face here and ending it," he briefly stopped speaking as he turned to face Nathan, "Before we try these bandits, have you any other questions for me?"

Nathan thought a moment, then spoke, "My Lord, a large brown wolf-beast accosted me on the way here amongst a pack of rabid dogs. Would that creature be an orcish pet? Its eyes were yellow and it was clearly smarter and more sadistic than the other dogs." Nathan felt a pang of adrenaline rush through him thinking of the beast that had nearly killed him. Thank goodness Saving Grace was there.

The king replied confidently, "Ah yes! They are known to keep a specific type of battle wolf and what you speak of fits their description. Nasty things, and a clear indication the orcs are involved in some way. If that is all, let us move on to trying these bandits!"

The king nodded at the halberdiers, who brought the bandits to their knees and removed their hoods. The men beneath looked more annoyed than afraid, and they also looked remarkably clean-cut for brigands. Nyland squinted at them slightly, as if he knew them.

"Hold Your Majesty, are these men not local merchants?" Nyland's surprise was evident on his face. He also seemed angry, but was clearly trying to suppress it in front of the king.

The halberdiers came around and examined the men, then voiced their agreement. "My King, I remember these men running stalls at the marketplace. It is strange they have resorted to becoming highwaymen," remarked a somewhat young-looking halberdier.

The king furrowed his brow and frowned, his stress creases reappearing momentarily on his forehead. "Hm, strange indeed. You two, you are accused of banditry and attempting to rob the merchant present here. Through two eyewitness accounts, I am inclined to believe these charges levied against you both carry weight and are truthful. What say you?"

One of the bandits, a man of about thirty with mutton chops and a thick moustache, began to speak somewhat sheepishly, "Forgive us, Your Highness, we had no other recourse. These animal raids have left many merchants in Kyrbor destitute by way of slowing trade in and out of the region to a crawl!"

The other bandit, a bit older and clean-shaven with a neat pony tail, chimed in sounding quite sorry as well, "Your Highness, we have sold our wares to you and your men before. We meant only to take what we thought wouldn't be missed. As merchants, we knew that bread was relatively worthless but exotic spice was incredibly valuable!

Ask Nyland, did we not leave the saffron and instead look with more interest upon the bread?"

The assembled men all looked to Nyland, and he nodded in agreement, though his countenance was stern. "Indeed, they did pay more attention to the bread than the saffron, though they also held me at knife-point and charged at Nathan when he intervened. That would hardly qualify them as innocent."

The king's gaze fell upon the bandits, and it was not one of mercy. "If this is true, and you are indeed violent highwaymen, it matters little if you left the more valuable wares alone. You still willingly used violence against innocents and that cannot stand! However, since you are former merchants and given the circumstances, I think we can reach an agreement. Rather than having you both thrown into the dungeon for banditry, if you accompany Nathan on his quest and help him in successfully resolving this animal matter, you will be exonerated. If you attack him or cause him to fail in his mission, you will hang. If you had no qualms about risking your lives for profit, then I see no issue in you risking them for glory. Do you agree to these terms?" The king glared at the two former merchants.

With little choice, the men reluctantly agreed. Armed as they were with short swords and leather armour, they'd be good scouts for Nathan, who was quite conspicuous and not at all stealthy in his shining plate armour. The halberdiers cut their bounds, and the two prisoners were given their weapons back. They looked a bit frightened at effectively becoming conscripts, but they also looked relieved at having avoided the noose, at least for the time being. Nyland didn't look particularly pleased, but he didn't seem willing to challenge the king.

"Well then, I would say the local Order hopes your progress is swift, but they are all off aiding another kingdom and will be away for quite some time. The only one left is the high priest and he's much too old to be off galivanting on the field of battle. The local guard is needed to protect our citizens from the animals, and I am needed here to deal with it all. I hope these merchants serve you well, as I fear it is about as much help as we can give you right now."

Nathan nodded, though he felt the king could have spared a halberdier or two. "Thank you, Your Majesty, I shall look into the matter and I shall not fail."

The king waved a hand to dismiss them, and the halberdiers lead Nathan, Nyland and the bandits out of the castle. Left at the front gates, their next order of business was to visit the smith and cartwright in the morning, as the setting sun made it clear that the shops were likely closed. They stopped at Nyland's home, both for him to drop off his wares and for him to get equipped to join them, as he decided this matter was of utmost importance and he had a duty to his city to help Nathan. His home had accommodations for four people, but he refused to open it up to bandits. Instead, Nyland pointed the way to an inn on the outskirts of the city and that is where they slept, ready to supply and prepare for what lay ahead on the morrow.

* * * * *

The next day, they dropped Nyland's wagon at the cartwright, though they wouldn't be bringing it along to the woods, and they dropped Nathan's plate mail at the blacksmith for repairs. The dents and dings could apparently be fixed quickly according to the smithy, and in that time, they decided to get the two bandits healed. Apparently, Nathan had concussed them, though Nyland was adamant they were lying. The high priest was honour-bound to give free healing to any member of the Order as well as anyone sponsored by a member of the Order, and since the bandits were technically the latter, he reluctantly healed them free of charge. The bandits thanked both Nathan and the high priest, though they glared somewhat accusingly at Nyland.

On the way out of the Order's temple, the bandits and Nyland began bickering about petty nonsense. Nyland felt they weren't trustworthy, and the bandits felt Nyland would actively work to see the bandits harmed or killed. The squabbling became rather rowdy, and Nathan had finally had it with them.

"Enough! All of you! Nyland's right to not trust you lot and you're right to suspect distrust on his part! Why would he trust the men who had just tried to rob him? You'll have to prove your loyalty to each other as we journey onwards, but I cannot let your petty squabbles jeopardize the quest before us!" All three men were taken aback, but not necessarily upset by Nathan's words. He was right, after all. "You two have to cooperate or you'll face the noose, and Nyland, you obviously want to protect your home and business. We can do it together, and I understand it won't be completely without friction, but our mission comes before our petty squabbles. We cannot have dissension within our own ranks!" Nathan thought he saw the high priest smiling out of the corner of his eye, but nobody was by the pillar of the temple when he looked.

Nyland sighed, but accepted the truth in Nathan's word. The bandits reluctantly agreed to behave themselves, though they asked they be referred to as Jeeves - the older man with the ponytail, and Kurtos - the younger one with the mutton chops and moustache. Everyone agreed to each other's terms, and the group was off. Nathan had been correct in more ways than one, as the high priest had indeed been watching. He watched the group walk off to the stables to fetch Saving Grace, and he was still smiling. Leadership and courage were exemplary traits within the Order, and the priest made a mental note of how capable Nathan had been at leading his group this day.

The group departed Kyrbor around noon, Nathan on horseback and the rest of them on foot. They'd gotten rations and other supplies while in town, and were now journeying onward to the forest as the king had bid them to. A few times they had seen a desperate looking animal, but it had run off swiftly anytime they got close. The dirt road began to become more overgrown as they reached the outskirts of the woods, and after a short while the path began to darken as the canopy above became thicker and thicker. The deeper into the forest they ventured, the fewer animals they saw as well. Once the path had given way entirely to forest, forcing Nathan to go it on foot and lead Saving Grace by its reins, there were no animals at all. Something was certainly forcing them from their woods, but what it was couldn't be ascertained yet.

The group had been quiet for most of their journey into the woods. The towering trees with dark green moss and lichen hanging off their branches and carpeting the ground, coupled with the eerie silence that permeated their surroundings, filled them all with dread.

Even Saving Grace seemed to feel it, because the horse nervously yanked on its reins and whinnied a few times, seemingly without cause. No deer ran by, no birds chirped, no bugs around to annoy them. Something was very off in the forest.

The sheer size of the forest and the lack of light made them lose track of time, but when the already dark woods became so dark that they were only able to see a few metres ahead, the group decided somewhat reluctantly to make camp as the beginnings of fatigue set in. A campfire provided some semblance of safety, but also the unnerving possibility that anything would be able to see their fire in the pitch-black and mossy woodlands. They all tried to push that thought away, but it lingered in the back of all of their minds.

"I've seen worse places. I once saw a town with open sewers and a raging plague going on. We're in relative luxury compared to that, eh?" Jeeves was clearly frightened but his attempt at humour was welcome.

"Yeah, yeah," Kurtos stuttered and fumbled his words a bit, "I'd say we're basically in a palace by comparison. It's a nice scenic area we're in and our camp is comfortable. I don't think we've seen a living thing yet, so we're probably safe." He didn't seem convinced of his own words.

Nyland was silent, but judging by his expression he was clearly nervous. Nathan decided he had to bolster their spirits. "Men, have heart and hold strong! We shall face nothing we cannot handle, and we have the sponsorship of both the king of Kyrbor and of my own kingdom! We shall prevail, and we shall succeed. I have no doubt of our abilities, and anything that gets in our way shall be defeated!" Quickly remembering what his king had said to him previously, he added, "Believe in yourselves as I do. We shall not fail!"

It seemed to help a little bit, and the men were at least at ease enough to rest. They kept watch in intervals, but nothing happened during the night. There were no sounds at all actually, not even an owl's hoot or the chirping of crickets. There was the occasional crackle of the fire, someone shifting or sighing in their sleep, but mostly there was absolute silence.

The next morning, after packing up their camp and setting out, Nathan thought it a good idea to send Jeeves and Kurtos ahead to scout while he and Nyland moved along with their supplies and Saving Grace behind them, both to break a trail to return back to Kyrbor and to ensure they don't accidentally move their supplies over rough terrain or into an enemy camp. The dark wood looked the same all around, and traversing it would take days. Without any animals around to cull it, the vegetation was overgrown and dense to the point finding a path through the vivid green leaves of shrubs and curtains of hanging moss was quite challenging.

For hours, nothing happened. Nyland and the bandits had come to an uneasy truce and ceased their bickering, but it would have been an almost welcome reprieve from the overwhelming and unnerving quiet. Hearing nothing but the occasional rustle of leaves or the snap of a twig underfoot as they marched forward put them all on edge. They all felt like a confrontation was always about to happen. Saving Grace was nervous as well, and had to be dragged along at times. At some point during their long march, the leaves overhead whispered pleasantly as a breeze rolled through the branches of the canopy above, but the sudden noise made all of them jump.

At some point into their journey, Jeeves and Kurtos crept back to Nathan, their faces white and their eyes wide with fear. The smell of a cooking fire hung in the air.

Jeeves nervously licked his lips as he spoke in a hushed but frantic tone, "Nathan, there are orcs ahead. I suggest Nyland stay out of sight with the horse, you go talk to them, and me and Kurtos take cover. When they inevitably attack you, we'll strike from ambush. They shouldn't have a chance to even get near us if all goes according to plan." Kurtos was silent, only quickly nodding his agreement through his frightened expression.

Nathan thought it cowardly to lurk in the bushes and attack from cover, but he wasn't about to risk the lives of his men. He reluctantly agreed, handing the reins of his horse to Nyland and unstrapping the shield on his back. The two bandits crept off as Nyland led Saving Grace back a bit and Nathan moved forward. Deep grunts and the crackle of fire became louder as Nathan moved forward through the brush, unperturbed by the poking branches and dense foliage because of his armour. Jeeves and Kurtos were a bit away on either side, creeping silently through the underbrush. It took a few minutes, but Nathan could soon see the glow of a campfire in the gloom of the woods, with several green-skinned orcs clad in leather armour and animal hides milling around it.

He quickly checked that both Jeeves and Kurtos were in position with their crossbows at the ready before moving in. He had his shield out but his sword sheathed, albeit his hand hovered over the pommel apprehensively as he advanced, clumsily and a little nervously, through the thick underbrush.

The orcs all turned to face him when he approached, though they didn't say anything or move towards him. They didn't even seem to be armed, which made Nathan move his hand away from the hilt of his sword somewhat. All their squinty eyes were upon him, until one who seemed to be a shaman judging by the headdress made of feathers and bones, broke the silence.

"What brings you here exalted one? By your insignia you're a Knight of the Order, and we have no quarrel with the forces of goodness as we are not a force of evil." Nathan's hand moved from his sword to his side. He didn't think they were going to attack.

"I come seeking the cause of the animal disturbances. I was attacked by one of your war wolves, thus I have just cause and the king's sponsorship to investigate your band." Nathan hoped this wouldn't turn hostile. He could feel himself begin to sweat in his armour.

The shaman nodded. "We, too, seek the cause of these disturbances. For many generations we've hunted in this forest and had great bounty. Now, as you can see, there is no game left. We had to set our dogs loose because they were going mad with hunger and attacking us, and that is why one accosted you. It was not our fault, at least not directly. We see now our actions may not have been without consequence for you humans, but we couldn't let our own pets turn on us." The other orcs grunted in agreement. Nathan was pretty sure they were telling the truth.

"If not you, then who or what is driving the animals away?" Nathan hoped they had the answer, because he wasn't terribly fond of the forest.

"Who, indeed," remarked the shaman, pausing to poke the fire with a nearby stick. "If the bones are to be believed, then I have divined the cause of the disturbances to be in the mountain not far from here. We are a group of volunteers who elected to plumb its caves and ascertain the cause of the disturbances. That's why we are few; the bones were clear something powerful is the cause and we didn't want to risk our whole tribe. Since we have a shared goal, perhaps we should join forces? You knights know tactics and combat, so with a contingent of our warriors lead by one such as you, we stand a fighting chance against any foe."

Nathan thought it over; on one hand the shaman had a point, though he doubted his men would willingly charge into combat beside orcs. He himself was apprehensive. "Possibly, though it seems odd you're so well-spoken. Have you been educated?" Nathan hoped that question didn't offend, though he wasn't sure it could be asked in a way that wouldn't.

The shaman sneered, bearing long teeth and purple gums. "You think we're ignorant savages? You think we live in the woods and have barbarous rituals and abduct children? We are not some stupid evil boogeymen! Some orcs are brutish, some are civilized, and some are quite intelligent. Just like you humans. It is reprehensible to imply we are lesser simply because we are orcs!" The other orcs were clearly offended by his statement as well. Nathan thought he saw one of the bandits raise a crossbow from the brush.

Thinking quickly before they took the shot, he shouted, "Jeeves! Kurtos! Nyland! Come out! The orcs have no hostile intentions!" There was a pause, then a rustling of leaves as the two bandits left their cover reluctantly. A clopping in the distance signalled Nyland was coming forward with Saving Grace. Nathan turned back to the orcish shaman. "I meant no offense; I was simply curious and had to be sure your band was no threat to my men. Obviously, I have judged you unfairly, and you and your band would prove invaluable in thwarting the evil we seek. Follow us, and together we shall expunge this vile force from these woods!" He really hoped his speech would rally everyone's morale.

The shaman thought it over, then nodded. "Very well. I am Gyrtrobog of the Wolf Clan and these are my men. Who are you?"

"I am Nathan Havarshire, here on the king's bidding to ascend as a full member of the Knight's Order. With me are Jeeves and Kurtos, bound to their mission under threat of the noose, and Nyland, a merchant seeking to protect his home and business from this evil. All of us have a vested interest in resolving this issue."

The orcs all grunted. "I see," said Gyrtrobog, seeming to think again, "I appreciate your candor. The mountain we seek is a journey of a day or two from here, and we should move out soon. Acquaint yourselves with the other men and help us pack up camp."

Nyland and Saving Grace, who were having some trouble getting through the brush, came into the clearing to see Jeeves and Kurtos helping orcs with their bedrolls and Nathan going over logistical plans with Gyrtrobog. He was glad the orcs were friendly, because how were four men and a horse going to stop a powerful evil if it proved to be much more than expected?

The journey after that was long, though at least the orcs proved to be surprisingly good company. They taught the humans their clan's stories and customs and Nathan regaled them with valiant tales of the Order. Nyland enjoyed talking about tinctures and fungus with Gyrtrobog, and the orcs were impressed by the stealth of Jeeves and Kurtos. What proved invaluable was the pathfinding the orcs possessed, and it sped their journey considerably knowing ways through the very thick vegetation. Saving Grace was especially happy about that!

They made camp at the end of the day, then marched again a full day, and again camped. Nothing seemed to happen until the end of the third day after the coalition of orcs and humans had formed. They were trekking through the wood, and noticed sunlight was beginning to poke through the dense canopy above. The more they walked towards the mountain, the brighter it became, and a reprieve from the gloom and darkness was most welcome! The sunlight became brighter and brighter, and the vegetation became less dense as well. Finally, they were out of the dark wood, and only a few scattered plants poked stubbornly from the ground. The group found themselves in a clearing, rejoicing at their progress. Gyrtrobog, however, was silent. The others came to see why as they looked around. The orcs looked a little silly all pale and saucer eyed, but it was no laughing matter. All around them were jagged and sharp tree stumps, poking through the earth like wickedly pointed teeth, evidence that this was once forest. In a massive circle that was miles wide around the mountain were tens of thousands of these jagged stumps, with the mountain itself looming above all the pointed nubs of trees, looking as ominous as ever among the remains of the enormous tract of cleared forest. It seemed this was why animals were retreating from the wood, as something was clearly destroying the forest on a large scale. Every member of the group got a sinking feeling in their stomachs. Nathan was glad to have a small army, because he would clearly need it.

Part 4

The group wasn't so merry anymore. It felt like they were marching through a necropolis, every jagged stump like a gravestone and the looming mountain like a great mausoleum, as the imaginations of everyone ran wild as to what exactly would be capable of such destruction and devastation in such a short span of time. Some of the orcs thought it was the work of vengeful spirits. Jeeves thought it to be a rogue lumber operation operating a hidden sawmill. There were whispers it was the work of a powerful monster that decided to lair in the mountain's deep caverns. Some said it was a manticore, some said it was an evil wizard. The most terrifying whispers were of a dragon, and that was why some of the stumps were charred ashes instead of jagged points. Either way, the mountain loomed ahead, but the thoughts and fears that ran through every human, orc and in Saving Grace's case, horse's, head left them feeling more terrified than triumphant.

The mountain itself was a day or two away by foot from where they had arrived in the bizarre clearing, mainly because of the extra time needed to carefully navigate the stumps. It was also odd nearly all the grass was either missing or burned away, leaving the entire area as barren dirt. Nathan carefully led Saving Grace amongst the stumps. His quest weighed heavily upon him. He must not fail in his duty, but exactly what creature would do this and why? Charred ashes and jagged tree stumps weren't exactly evil's go to modus operandi, and he was truly frightened by the possibility he was marching right into death's door to fight an impossibly strong beast against which he could not possibly prevail.

Jeeves and Kurtos had nowhere to hide, and little cause to scout the wide-open expanse of jagged points and tracts of dirt, yet they still broke the path ahead alone, mainly out of habit than necessity. The orcs followed behind, clearing the path by hacking at the stumps with their battle axes, while Nathan, Nyland and Gyrtrobog along with Saving Grace were at the back of the contingent with their supplies.

Beyond hushed whispers of what they were about to face, there wasn't much in the way of conversation. Nyland was silent, no surprise there, but Nathan had hoped that Gyrtrobog would've been more talkative. It wasn't clear if the orcish shaman had real abilities or if it was all simply a position of honour and prestige, but Nathan assumed a shaman must possess strong intuition at the very least. While the contingent marched on, hacking at stumps and looking around fearfully, Nathan decided to see what Gyrtrobog's thoughts were.

He looked to the shaman, in his feathered headdress adorned with bones, his painted and tattooed face being very hard to read. It was difficult to tell if he was frightened or pensive.

"Gyrtrobog? What do the bones foretell of our coming battle?"

Gyrtrobog jumped a bit, looking to Nathan with a bewildered expression. "Hm? Oh yes, yes. They tell of a powerful being, one capable of destruction on a grand scale, though not one without reason." His face still had an unreadable expression.

Nathan mulled it over for a moment or two, then remarked, "So in theory we could just talk to it if the bones are to be believed? Perhaps whatever it is we face isn't aware of the destruction it's caused?"

Gyrtrobog seemed surprised, and his face softened considerably, "I hadn't thought of that. We've been dreading this encounter this whole time when it may be as simple as a bit of diplomacy with a powerful being. Hm, we shall see soon enough, the mountain looms before us," Nathan followed Gyrtrobog's gaze and indeed they had reached just outside the foot of the mountain, "And here is where we shall camp. Tomorrow, we uncover the cause of all this."

Nathan nodded in agreement and shouted to the men to make camp. Everyone felt incredibly on edge; the evil they were to vanquish was only a mile or two away from them, hidden in the mountain towering above. The mountain itself looked even more ominous now that they were so close; it was a stone point jutting from the earth pocked all over with cave openings. They made camp, but were too scared to make a fire and risk alerting whatever evil was in there of their presence. Nobody ate much either. An uneasy, fretful rest marked the transition from dusk to dawn, and though they were dreading the inevitable confrontation, they marched forward to the mountain.

The closer they got, the more the land was simply flat dirt or scorched earth. The jagged tree stumps were missing entirely, and the sense of foreboding was only amplified by the howls and echoes loudly emitting from the caverns ahead. It took an hour, but they had reached the steep mountain's base, and before them were innumerable cave entrances. Some were so shallow that the end could be seen from the entrance, but a few of them were completely dark only a couple feet in, and loud echoes came from deep within many of them.

The contingent froze in place. No one knew how to proceed, nor did anyone really want to. Nathan was just as terrified as his men, but he wasn't going to let fear stop him from completing his quest when he had come so far already.

"All of you, stay here. I'll scout ahead with a torch and report back," said Nathan with only a hint of fear in his voice as he motioned for one of the orcs to hand him one.

"We shall go too, these caves should be good for sneaking," remarked Kurtos as he and Jeeves unbuckled their crossbows from their backs and began loading them.

Gyrtrobog stepped forward too, "I shall be going as well. The rest of you stay here, I figure four of us in an expeditionary squad should give a fighting chance against whatever we find." He was a bit scared, but he was also a warrior-shaman with a duty to his tribe.

The torches were lit as they entered the biggest and deepest opening. By the dim light of the torch and what little sunlight filtered in, it seemed to be a long tunnel with openings on all sides, even the floor and ceiling. They cautiously moved forward, being incredibly careful to watch every step. There was no telling how deep the jet-black openings were, and falling into one could mean a drop to one's death.

The echoes and howls within seemed to mostly be the wind blowing throughout the many caverns and cave openings, though there were sounds that seemed to be loud growls somewhere deeper in the cave. It made them all anxious.

The further in they went, the further the pin-prick of light that marked the way out became. The rocky floor of the cave seemed to have deep scratch marks in many areas, most of them longer than a man is tall. Every mark seemed to lead down the main corridor rather than into the adjoining holes. Gyrtrobog suggested all the various holes and side-caverns may be there simply as decoys.

They were terrified moving forward, and incredibly on edge. The faint dripping of water somewhere was a constant sound that brought them no comfort, and while the howls and echoes had died down where they were, the growls seemed to grow louder and louder.

The trek through the enormous cavern couldn't have taken more than a half-hour, but navigating the floor filled with holes and the feelings of dread made it all seem much longer. The tiny point of light far in the distance was their only reminder the outside world still existed, and hadn't been replaced entirely by darkness and fear.

Eventually, the growls were all that could be heard, and the corridor they had been walking down opened up into a massive cavern. Jeeves and Kurtos volunteered to explore it and report back with what they found. Nathan thought it was so they could point to this moment if it were ever to be called into question how they helped on the quest, but he wasn't about to stop them. They crept into the cavern silently, with only their torches making slight crackling sounds to give away their position, though the sounds were muffled by the growls. They went a short way in, then stopped abruptly.

Their torches partially illuminated the cavern, and the light was reflecting off a shiny, metallic surface. At first, it seemed like metal or jewels gleaming in the torchlight, but it was the scaly nature of the reflective material that made that an impossibility. They moved their torches, with Kurtos fumbling and dropping his with a clatter, but not before it illuminated the thing in the cave's giant head. The majestic horns, the scaled hide and the toothy maw betrayed its identity. The growls belonged to this sleeping dragon, and it was absolutely colossal! It was easily the size of a castle, and they were basically right beside it!

Terror gripped all four of them. Nobody knew what to do. It was made much, much worse when the growling stopped. A scraping of claws on stone and some grunting made them all wide-eyed and possessed by the most powerful fear they had ever felt. The dragon was awake, and they were just standing there, holding torches or looking at it gob smacked with their mouths agape. They were going to die, and they were going to die looking like confused fish.

A jet of flames erupted upwards from the beast's nostrils, briefly illuminating its gigantic form in the darkness, though mercifully its back was turned. Running away seemed to be impossible since the floor was pocked with cave openings, and there was no way they could fight this colossal creature. Gyrtrobog looked to Nathan, and although they could barely see each other, there was a look in Gyrtrobog's eyes besides just terror. He nodded his head slightly towards the dragon, and Nathan knew what he had to do. He really hoped the bones were correct and this beast could be reasoned with.

He'd never been more scared in his life, his armour felt so heavy and he wanted so badly to just flee. He took a clumsy step forward, then another. Fear had no place in a knight's heart, and Nathan's only option here was to talk to it. He took a deep breath, hoped it wasn't his last, and spoke. "Hail dragon, we have stumbled upon your lair by accident, and ask you allow us passage so we may find the cause of strife on behalf of our kingdoms."

There was no answer. They stood there, petrified with terror, with a dragon now knowing there were intruders in its cave. After a couple seconds, though of course to the four men it felt like an eternity, there came a reply spoken in an oddly unthreatening voice, "Why hello! Pardon my manners, I've just awoken and feel a bit hazy. I am Ethyloch the Great, vegetarian and proud dragon! You may look at me with awe, I don't mind. Here, allow me to illuminate the cave so you may gaze upon me and be properly starstruck," he said as a bright column of flame erupted from his mouth, catching a nearby stack of tree trunks on fire. The blazing pile was sufficient enough to light up the cave, a rather circular and high-ceilinged cave, and of course Ethyloch. He was still the size of a small castle, though in better lighting he looked a lot less menacing. He looked downright friendly! His eyes were golden, and shone with kindness rather than malice; his scales shone in the light in such a way that it was like rainbows washed over him, though in the moments between the effect he seemed to have green scales.

"Hail Ethyloch! I am Nathan Havarshire, here to solve the crisis of the animals attacking Kyrbor! With me are Jeeves and Kurtos, men honour-bound to aid me by the king, and Gyrtrobog, a shaman of an orcish tribe affected by the same problems as Kyrbor. Do you know what the cause is, oh Great One?" Nathan's terror was quickly replaced with awe. Ethyloch was truly a stunning creature to behold.

Ethyloch seemed amused, then his expression changed to a sheepish one. "Uh, yes. I think I might have done that. Not on purpose, I assure you, it's just when a dragon moves in other creatures tend to move out. I came to this mountain a month or two ago looking for a quiet spot to make my lair, and as I am vegetarian, I suppose eating the forest may have contributed to the creatures fleeing. No doubt you saw the tree stumps? I sometimes even eat the grass and stumps to conserve food but I guess a dragon eats a lot, at least compared to what you humans and orcs do." He seemed to be genuinely sorry.

Nathan thought a moment, then had an amazing idea pop into his head! "Wait, you're vegetarian you said? What would you think of eating wheat instead of trees? Kyrbor has an abundance of wheat to the point most of it goes to waste. If you moved from here to nearby Kyrbor, perhaps between that kingdom and my own, you could eat as much wheat as you wanted! If we ever ran low, you could simply eat the grass or trees of the plains! We could solve the animal problem, you could be an honorary member of both kingdoms, and everybody's happy! We'd have to discuss it with the kings, of course, but wouldn't that be grand?"

Ethyloch grinned wide, and he had to agree, it did sound lovely. The orcs and animals would get their forest back, Ethyloch would get free food and attention forever and be a major boon to both kingdoms as well, because after all, how many kingdoms could count a dragon as part of their citizenry? He agreed to arrive outside Kyrbor in two weeks' time, which would allow Nathan to return to Kyrbor and tell the king the news as well as have a messenger run to Nathan's own kingdom. The four men departed in good spirits, and when they rejoined their contingent, there were cheers of victory. They had triumphed, not only in fixing the problem, but in making friends with a dragon!

Two weeks passed, and both kings had arrived on the outskirts of Kyrbor. Jeeves and Kurtos were there, now merchants once again, as they had succeeded in aiding Nathan and had been exonerated. Nyland was happy that his home and business were secure, and the populace was thrilled the animals had begun returning back to the forest. The orcs were absent from the gathering, but they, too, were incredibly grateful for the help of the humans and had pledged their assistance if ever it was needed. Nathan's leadership and bravery had been noted, and already he was a full-fledged member of the Knights of the Order. His success in the mission was so incredible that he had been celebrated as a hero, and he had almost never had to use violence to be one! The matter was not completely over yet, however, as the dragon still hadn't made an appearance. Once it had been spoken to, then all would be put to rest. Ethyloch had gone to live with his brother while they prepared, and was due at Kyrbor today, at this exact time.

The gathered people watched the skies in anticipation, and when a great green dragon appeared on the horizon, inspiring both awe and fear in the people assembled, they knew that soon the matter would be put to rest.

Ethyloch landed gracefully in an empty field; he was so enormous that even the tallest spire of Castle Kyrbor was dwarfed by his size. Still, his golden eyes were devoid of ill will, and the townspeople were quickly put at ease. The dragon talked to the kings, and Nathan, and then the kings again, and it was decided what was to happen. Ethyloch would live in a great quarry that had been used to provide the stone to build several castles long ago, conveniently between the two kingdoms. He would help clear fields and forests to build things, and would be paid in wheels of cheese and as much wheat as he could eat. Lastly, he would serve as a protector of both cities. Ethyloch happily agreed.

So ends the tale of Nathan the Knight. A nervous squire became a brave and confident knight, not through waging war, and not through thinking really, really hard without taking action. No, he did it by swallowing his fear, leading those around him to victory, and never shying away from confronting what he had to, no matter how hard it was. As for the two kingdoms, they flourished after Ethyloch took up residence between them. He became a tourist attraction, and given how much dragons love to be admired and fawned over, Ethyloch was quite pleased that people came from far and wide to see Ethyloch the Great, vegetarian dragon and guardian of two kingdoms. He also sometimes ate a forest or cleared a plain of grass for construction purposes, but mostly he was a tourist attraction. Nathan served well as a member of the Order, Kyrbor was saved, and Ethyloch was a boon to both kingdoms while he himself lived a luxurious and happy existence. Nathan had more than succeeded on his quest, and his name was sung on high for centuries afterward.

Made in the USA
Las Vegas, NV
09 January 2025

91843e0e-a826-40ee-98b6-c152e9f5660fR03